"Why are you on the rodeo circuit if you love ranch work so much?"

Joel's hand closed over hers. "It seems contradictory, doesn't it?"

April couldn't concentrate on what he said. Her mind focused on where his hand surrounded hers. As hard as she tried to understand, her mind had gone on overload. "Uh, yes."

His gaze locked with hers and he slowly lowered his head toward her.

The screen door slammed, bursting the bubble surrounding them. The boys stood on the porch.

"Could you come inside and say good-night, Mr. Joel, before you leave?" Saved by a screen door. Her heart beat so hard she thought it would jump out of her chest.

His gaze didn't move from her face for several moments. He broke the connection and looked at the boys. "Of course I'll come in and say good-night."

He leaned down and whispered, "I'll be back."

April watched as her boys waited on Joel. It stole her breath. They were so eager to have a man's time and attention.

But what would the boys do when Joel was gone?

Leann Harris has always had stories in her head. Once her youngest child went to school, she began putting those stories on a page. She is active in her local RWA chapter and ACFW chapters. She's a teacher of the deaf (high school), a master composter and avid gardener, and teaches writing at her local community college. Her website is leannharris.com.

Books by Leann Harris

Love Inspired

Rodeo Heroes

A Ranch to Call Home
A Rancher for Their Mom

Second Chance Ranch
Redemption Ranch
Fresh-Start Ranch

Love Inspired Suspense

Hidden Deception
Guarded Secrets

Visit the Author Profile page at Harlequin.com for more titles.

A Rancher
for Their Mom

Leann Harris

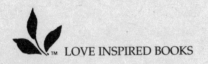 LOVE INSPIRED BOOKS

Recycling programs
for this product may
not exist in your area.

ISBN-13: 978-0-373-81845-7

A Rancher for Their Mom

Copyright © 2015 by Barbara M. Harrison

www.Harlequin.com

Printed in U.S.A.

Your love, Lord, endures forever—
do not abandon the works of Your hands.
—*Psalms* 138:8

This book has been a journey for me.
I want to thank the editors at Love Inspired for
their help and support, particularly my editor,
Shana Asaro. Her guidance has been invaluable.
And I want to thank Dr. Nandita Rao, the nurses
and technicians at Texan Oncology
for their support and wonderful smiles
while I was going through chemotherapy.

And my Sunday School class,
the ladies in my Bible study, and my family
and friends who brought meals.
I did not go through this cancer alone.

Chapter One

"Mom, Mom," six-year-old Todd yelled, the back screen door slamming against its frame. The sound of little cowboy boots pounded through the kitchen and down the hall. "Where are you, Mom?"

"I'm in the office," April Landers answered.

The screen slammed again, followed by another set of small boot falls. April winced, hoping the boys didn't wake their younger sister from her nap.

Breathless, Todd appeared in the doorway. "Wes told me no one born in February could be a cowboy. Only boys born in June could be cowboys. That's not true, is it?"

Eight-year-old Wes appeared behind his brother, a smirk on his face. April's brow arched as her gaze engaged her older son. His grin disappeared.

"I can be a cowboy, too, can't I?" Todd pleaded.

"Opa and your cousin Chad have birthdays in February. Weren't they cowboys?"

Todd's frown disappeared and his eyes widened. "Yes." He turned to his brother and stuck out his tongue.

Wes's expression went from somber to a grin. He shrugged.

"Ha, you're wrong. I can be a cowboy, too." Todd stomped back down the hall.

Wes turned to follow his brother.

"Stop, young man."

Wes halted, his shoulders hunching.

April pushed away from the antique desk. "Come here."

He looked up and she motioned her son to her side. Wes dragged his feet as if going to an execution and stopped when he got to her knees. He refused to raise his head.

"Wes, look at me."

Her son slowly raised his head.

"Why did you tell your brother he couldn't be a cowboy?"

He shrugged his shoulders, kicking an imaginary piece of dirt on the floor.

April sighed. She knew her boys missed Opa—their grandfather Vernon—who had died last September. "Do you think Opa would've liked you telling that story to your brother?"

He hung his head. "No. He wouldn't have liked it."

"I didn't like it, either. I'm disappointed with you."

Wes's lips pursed.

"Come closer."

He moved and April drew him into her arms and hugged him. All sorts of emotions bounced around her chest.

The boys needed a male figure in their lives to help and guide them since Opa's death. Their father had died in an oil platform accident over three years ago. April's own father couldn't fill the role, since he still worked on an oil platform out in the Gulf. He was the manager and only made it back to shore once every six months.

"I don't want you to lie to your brother again. He looks up to you."

Wes scuffed his boot. "I was just playing."

"Would you like some of the older boys at school to tease you like that?"

He shook his head.

"You can go outside and play if you boys have finished your chores."

Wes pursed his lips. "We were almost finished when Todd told me he wanted to be a cowboy like Jimmy Rogers's dad. You know that Jimmy's dad is going to compete in the rodeo next week?

Could we go? Please?" His eyes filled with hope and longing.

"We'll see."

His expression fell and his lower lip jutted out. "'Kay."

Wes's posture, slumped shoulders and dragging feet tore at her heart.

The rodeo was in town, but the competition would take place next weekend. April wished she had the extra money to buy tickets to take the boys to see it. It just wasn't in the budget. Money was tight, which was why she'd decided to sell the two horses her father-in-law had raised for the rodeo. They were a little young, and if she could've held out until December, it would've been better, but she couldn't afford the extra money needed for the horses' upkeep.

Even with the money woes and problems the ranch faced, she wouldn't change a thing about her life—except having her late husband's vision of the future match hers. With all the traveling her family had done as she was growing up, this little piece of Texas in the Panhandle was her ideal spot. Roots. A place to belong. Waking up every day in the same place. That was paradise.

Ross had never understood that need for a home she could live in 24/7, 365 days a year. "Lord, I'm feeling a little overwhelmed here. Could You send me some help?"

The baby cried, alerting April that her few minutes of reprieve were over.

Joel Kaye turned his truck and the rodeo's horse trailer down the private road of the Circle L Ranch. At the end of the gravel drive stood a single-story white clapboard ranch house, with a deep front porch that shaded the house in the late afternoon and a porch swing that swayed in the breeze. A faded red barn stood to the right of the house, opening onto a large area where an old truck was parked.

Like the lightning strike that had taken out the electronics at his family's ranch a couple of springs ago, a longing for home shot through him, leaving him off balance. Shaking off the weird feeling, Joel pulled to a stop before the barn entrance. By the time he slammed the truck door shut, two little boys had barreled out of the barn's double doors and skidded to a stop. They looked at him, then each other.

"Hello, I'm looking for Mrs. April Landers."

The boys eyed him, making Joel feel like a horse ready to be auctioned.

"That's our mom," the taller boy answered. "Do you want to talk to her?"

"I do. Could you get her?"

The boy cupped his hands around his mouth and yelled, "Mom, there's someone out here who wants to talk to you!"

Joel fought back a grin. That wasn't exactly how he'd expected the boy to get his mother, but Joel understood.

Their sharp gazes roamed over him, and Joel saw the questions on their faces. They looked at the horse trailer beside him.

"You with the rodeo?" the older child asked.

They huddled together, waiting.

"I am."

"What do you do?" the older boy asked.

"I help around the rodeo with chores. I also compete in events."

"What events?"

"Calf roping, bareback riding and steer wrestling."

"When's your birthday?" the younger boy piped up, stepping forward.

Joel's brow wrinkled. "March. I had a birthday last week." He'd turned thirty-four and felt every day of his age.

The younger boy turned to his brother. "See, you're wrong." His words were a singsong *na, na, na.* He moved to Joel's side. "What's your name?"

Joel squatted to get eye level with the boy. "My name is Joel Kaye. What's yours?"

"I'm Todd and that's my brother, Wes, who doesn't know nothin'."

Obviously, Joel had landed in the midst of an argument. "It's nice to meet you."

"What are you doing here?" Todd persisted.

"I'm here to talk to your mom."

"Why?" Wes demanded.

"Do you do bull riding?" Todd asked, scooting closer, leaving Joel no time to answer his brother's question.

Holding up his hand, Joel motioned for quiet. "I'll answer your questions, but I need to talk to your mom."

"Mom," the older boy bellowed again.

The boys seemed to vibrate with excitement.

"So, are you two rodeo fans?"

Their heads moved like bobblehead dolls.

"I love the bareback riding," Todd added, his eyes filled with eagerness. "And bull riding."

"You've got to be mighty strong to ride those bulls," Joel warned. His first time on the circuit he'd tried bull riding and caught a hoof on his upper arm and had six stitches. Now he only rode horses.

Todd's eyes widened. "I know, but I can. I do calf scramble now."

"I'm impressed." Joel remembered the first time he'd managed to rope the gatepost of the corral behind his family's barn. He'd been about Todd's age and his father had witnessed the event.

The back door slammed, bringing his attention to the woman exiting the house. Several strands of her soft brown hair, piled on her head, hung around her face, giving her the look of a woman who cared for and chased after small children. Tall and slender, there was a quiet strength in her that drew him, something none of the flashy women hanging around the rodeo had. She had a little girl riding on her hip.

Joel stood and tipped his hat to her. "Ma'am, Joel Kaye. I'm here to pick up the horses you wanted to sell to the rodeo."

"Mom, you're not going to sell our horses, are you?" Wes asked, racing to her side. A note of fear laced his voice.

"No, I'm not going to sell Buckwheat and Sammie."

His rigid posture eased.

"I'm selling Sadie and Helo. You know Opa planned on selling them to the rodeo."

Todd's posture didn't ease, broadcasting his distrust.

"Really?" Wes eyed his mother.

April cupped her son's chin. "Really. Your grandfather gave you Buckwheat. He's yours, and Sammie is your brother's horse. I will not sell them."

Wes studied her. "Okay."

Turning to Joel, she waved him forward. "C'mon, I'll show you where the horses are."

"Did you know he calf ropes in the rodeo?" Todd hurried after his mother. "And his birthday is in March," Todd added, sticking his nose up in a see-I-told-you-so-attitude.

Joel caught her smile.

"It's a long story." She turned and walked to the corral behind the barn and pointed out the black horse with the star on her forehead and the tan horse with a darker brown mane and two front stockings. "Sadie and Helo are the two my father-in-law thought would work well in the rodeo."

Her words sent his mind off in a different direction. Her father-in-law. Jack Murphy had told him that the Landerses had supplied animals for the rodeo for several years.

"I hadn't planned on selling them so soon, but the drought being as severe as it has been, I couldn't afford to keep them another six months."

The little girl in April's arms smiled at Joel and shyly laid her head on her mother's shoulder.

He winked at her and she turned her face in to her mother's body.

"Well, I know Jack is glad to have the stock. I'll go get some halters out of the trailer." The boys huddled around their mother.

"Can I help?" Todd asked, coming out from behind his mother's leg.

April visibly tensed.

"Of course. I could use some help."

A sigh of relief escaped her. Todd beamed and followed Joel to the trailer. As they were walking away, Joel paused and waved Wes toward them. "I could use your help, too. I have two halters, one for each horse."

Wes's face lit. "Okay." He looked at his mother. "I'm going to help."

April's stance eased and she smiled. "I heard, and I know you can help, too." Beaming with pride, Todd and Wes trailed behind Joel.

Thank you, she mouthed.

Joel nodded. Together they moved to the trailer. He opened the back door and walked into the divided interior. Two ropes sat on the floor. Joel handed each boy a rope and watched as they slipped them up their arms, holding the coiled ropes close.

Joel left the doors to the trailer open. "Okay, guys, let's go get those horses." The boys grinned at him and followed.

Hearing the boys walking behind him brought a smile to Joel's lips. His gaze collided with April's. Her expression, a curious mixture of caution and appreciation, caught him off guard. Did she think he'd be cruel to her boys? Ignore them? But then again, she didn't know him from Adam. Joel found himself admiring the mama bear, determined to protect her cubs.

"How contrary are the horses?" Joel threw the question over his shoulder.

"They're not broken, but both can be won over with a carrot."

He stopped and turned to her. "Good idea. Do you have some?"

"Some?" Her brain short-circuited.

"Carrots."

April's cheeks heated and she felt dumber than dirt. "Yeah, I'll get them." She turned toward the kitchen with Cora still cradled in her arms. The toddler protested and held out her arms to the cowboy. April stared down at her daughter. "Sweetie, he doesn't want to hold you." She turned toward the house, but Cora put up a fuss.

April frowned at her daughter's behavior. Lately, Cora wasn't willing to let any stranger near her.

"I don't mind holding her while you get the carrots."

Joel's words startled her. He didn't look frightened or uncomfortable about holding the two-and-a-half-year-old.

Cora leaned toward the tall cowboy, still holding out her arms. He wrapped his hands around her daughter and settled her close to his chest.

Cora batted her lashes at him, instantly winning him over. April struggled to keep her mouth from falling open. Suddenly her picky daughter decided to be friendly.

"I think we've got everything under control here, except for the carrots."

The stupor that held April in place evaporated. She turned and hurried into the kitchen. What was going on? Suddenly her children had latched on to this stranger while she acted like a teenager, with her heart fluttering in excitement. She wasn't that green anymore.

Grabbing the carrots out of the refrigerator, April fought to regain her balance. She'd just prayed for some help, but surely he wasn't it. God knew her hurts and past, and this cowboy fit none of her needs. Joel worked for the traveling rodeo, which was in a different city each week. He probably had that same wandering gene her father and husband had had. She'd had enough of *that* and wanted nothing to do with a man who couldn't commit to one place.

Hurrying outside, she stopped short when she saw all three of her children surrounding Joel, talking to him. They looked so perfect together. Just looking at the group, one would never know the children weren't his.

It stole her breath.

The sound of the screen door slamming brought everyone's attention to her.

"Here are the carrots." She held them up and hurried down the side steps, shaking off her fantasies. Obviously, she'd been alone too long and any help she got was bound to throw her off stride.

But I prayed.

Arriving beside Joel, April held out her arms for Cora. Her daughter didn't budge.

"C'mon, sweetie."

Cora didn't respond.

April felt her cheeks grow hot. She smiled and plucked Cora out of Joel's arms. "If you're half as good with horses as you are with kids, Sadie and Helo shouldn't be any problem for you."

The tall cowboy smiled slowly. "I'm better."

She swallowed hard. *Oh, my.*

Joel took the carrots and walked to the corral gate.

"What are you goin' to do?" Todd asked, following Joel. "Are you going to rope Helo and Sadie?"

"I'm going to make friends with a couple of nervous horses." He held out his hand and took the ropes from Wes and Todd, hanging them over the gatepost. He opened the gate and walked inside but made no move toward the horses. Helo and Sadie nervously moved to the other side of the corral.

The boys crowded around the gate, hanging on to the horizontal brace. April moved behind them.

"Sometimes you just have to let a horse get to know you." He placed one carrot in his back pocket and held out the other one. "Let them feel you, catch your scent."

"Is that why you're just standing there doing nothin'?" Wes asked. "I thought you'd charge in there and rope the horses."

"I could, but if I came into your house and started demanding things from you, you wouldn't like it, would you?"

Todd's face screwed up as he thought. "No."

"Horses are the same."

"Oh."

The horses stilled as Joel waited, but curiosity won out and the black horse moved closer to him. Joel held up the carrot, waving it around. Slowly the black horse drifted toward him. Joel held the carrot still, and the horse accepted it.

"Sadie's eating it," Todd whispered.

Joel rubbed the horse's forehead, then ran his hand down her neck. She accepted his touch. As he worked to win the horse's trust, he felt the gazes of the boys and their mother on him. Their interest and admiration warmed him in a way that surprised him.

It took less than ten minutes for Joel to win Sadie's trust, and she allowed him to slip the rope over her head.

"Wow," the boys whispered.

Joel slowly led Sadie out of the corral to his trailer. He paused at the tailgate. The boys peered at him, their little bodies tense. Sadie only paused a moment before she walked into the trailer.

"How'd you do that?" Todd demanded.

"When you do something that isn't familiar to you, you're nervous, right? It's the same for horses." Joel glanced at April and found admiration on her face, too. It was common sense, but his heart soaked up her reaction.

It took less time for him to coax Helo to his side, and he slipped the rope over his head. When he had both horses secured in the trailer, he turned to the two boys.

"Are y'all comin' to the rodeo next weekend?"

The kids turned to their mother with pleading expressions. They were good, Joel admitted to himself. They could put the hurt on anyone.

"Can we?"

Joel saw the answer in April's bleak face. That was why she was selling her horses early.

"We'll see."

"But, Mom," Todd whined.

The woman tilted her head and her eyes narrowed.

Nothing else was said.

Joel pulled his truck around and headed out.

As he drove back to the rodeo, Joel's heart ached. He understood the woman's pride that she could take care of her own. He only wished there was something he could do to help.

Later that afternoon, Joel drove into the parking lot of the Caprock Feed & Seed store to pick up extra feed for the rodeo. On his way back from this feed run, he might stop by the Dairy Queen he'd spotted and have a chicken-fried steak burger.

Entering the store, Joel saw April talking to the clerk. He didn't spot either of the boys, but Cora stood by her mother, holding April's leg.

"So, Sully, what do you recommend I plant in the other fields, beside the hay for my own animals?"

He hadn't noticed earlier how musical her voice sounded. Now he knew he'd be haunted by it when he laid his head down tonight.

"I know you don't want to plant cotton like the majority of the farms around here, but you could try a field of wheat, soybeans or sorghum. Manufacturers want sweet sorghum for syrup," the clerk said.

"Or you could try planting sunflowers." The words popped out of Joel's mouth before he thought.

April jerked and turned toward him. "Sunflowers?"

"Mr. Joel," Todd yelled in excitement, darting out from behind a tall pile of sacks of feed.

Wes followed and hurried to Joel's side. Cora made a beeline to him.

He picked her up and she patted him on the chest.

"Mr. Joel."

Joel's heart melted at the munchkin's twinkling eyes. When he looked up, a frown wrinkled April's brow. Was her expression from him holding Cora or the advice he'd given?

"Sunflowers are a good cash crop. Several of the farms and ranches around my family's ranch started growing them. The crop requires little work and when harvested, there are multiple places to sell them."

The clerk's stare bored into Joel.

"I'm Joel Kaye." He stuck out his hand.

"He's with the rodeo, Mr. Sully," Todd helpfully announced. "He knows how to throw a lariat and has a birthday in March and is a cowboy."

Sully shook Joel's hand.

"Jack sent me here for the feed he ordered."

The man's attitude changed. "It's ready, but let me finish with Mrs. Landers first."

"That's okay, Sully. I need to think about your suggestions on what to plant."

Sully nodded. "Drive around back and we'll load the order." He disappeared into the back.

"I didn't mean to butt in." Joel stepped closer to the counter. April's hair fell around her face, tempting him to reach out and touch the shiny rich brown strands.

"No, I appreciate it. I've been wondering what to do with the fields my father-in-law normally cultivated. Sunflowers. I hadn't thought of that."

"I wouldn't have, either, but as I told you several of my neighbors planted them as a cash crop and they liked the results."

Sully appeared again. "It's ready."

Joel didn't know whether to laugh or scowl at Sully's impatience. When Joel tried to put Cora down, she protested. April took her daughter from his arms and hushed the girl. Joel nodded and walked outside to his truck.

He drove around the building and backed his truck up to the loading dock. Sully helped Joel transfer the bags of feed from the wooden pallet into the truck. Halfway through, the boys appeared on the dock.

Sully looked at the pair. "Y'all here to help?"

"We're too small," Todd answered. They carefully watched and whispered to each other.

Once they finished loading, Sully drove the small forklift back into the warehouse.

Joel opened the truck door.

"Mr. Joel," Wes began.

Joel stopped and turned toward the boys.

After a couple of intense whispers, Wes walked forward. "After you left this morning, Mr. Moore, the man who helps Mom with the ranch, got hurt. She called the ambulance for him. He can't work for a while. We heard Mom crying after the ambulance left."

"And praying," Todd added.

Wes's solemn gaze locked with Joel's. "Mom's real worried about the ranch."

Todd's head nodded in agreement.

Like a shot to his gut, the boys' words hit Joel

hard. The worry in their eyes would've touched the hardest of hearts.

Wes took a deep breath. "We want to hire you to help Mom plant her fields."

Todd's head bobbed. "Yeah, we want to hire you."

Joel hadn't seen that one coming. "I'm still with the rodeo, boys."

Todd's shoulders straightened. "But are you working this week? You're having spring break like we are. Don't the animals have spring break, too? Won't you have time?"

Spring break? Joel's eyes widened. Well, he'd just complained to Hank about all the downtime he had on his hands this week with nothing to do.

They waited.

Todd reached into his pocket and pulled out some change. Wes followed by taking out of his front pocket a crumpled dollar and three pennies. "We have a dollar and thirty-seven cents between Todd and me that we can pay you."

"Is that enough?" Todd's face filled with longing and uncertainty.

Talk about being caught off guard. But how could he ignore such an honest plea? Joel swallowed hard. "I still would have to help feed the animals at the rodeo in the morning—"

The boys nodded.

"—but if that's okay with you, I'd be proud to work for two such upstanding cowboys."

"And our mom."

"Most certainly."

They beamed and Todd started to jump up and down.

"Okay. Let me take the feed back to the rodeo, then I'll drive out to your place and talk with your mom to make sure it's all right with her."

"Okay."

The boys stepped forward and dumped their money into Joel's hand. Looking at the crumpled bill and coins, he felt the most unusual emotions—hope and satisfaction. When he glanced up, he saw two excited faces.

"I'll see you in a bit."

Driving away, Joel shook his head and chuckled. Who would've thought those two young boys would come up with such an ingenious plan? He hadn't. But what mattered most was how their mother felt. And oddly enough, he wasn't sure April would accept his help. He wondered if those boys could work their charm on their mother as well as him. That he wanted to see.

Chapter Two

April kicked the front tire of the cantankerous tractor. What was wrong with this miserable piece of equipment? How could she plow the west field for hay or the north field for sunflowers if the tractor wouldn't start?

"Is there a problem?"

April jerked around, coming face-to-face with Joel. He grinned, making her knees weak. *Stop it.* Ignoring her crazy feelings, she said, "I've got an uncooperative piece of machinery. I've watched my father-in-law coax this ancient thing into starting several times. Of course, Vernon did most of the plowing." But at this point, she didn't have an option. A noise at the barn doors drew her attention. The boys stood there, watching.

"Do you mind if I try?"

Stepping to the side, she motioned for Joel to go ahead. "No. It might cooperate with you better than me."

The boys snickered, and Joel laughed. The wonderful, rich sound eased her heart.

"I don't know, but I've worked with some mighty grumpy equipment, and you have to know just how to coax them to life."

"You mean a wrench up the side of this thing won't work?" She ran her fingers through her hair, dislodging the clip holding it back.

"My gramps used that technique, and it worked, but let me look at the motor and see if I can find the problem. And if that doesn't work, we'll try your plan B, which is a wrench up the side of this thing." His eyes twinkled, and she heard the boys snicker.

Joel's humor found her funny bone and she joined in with everyone's light spirit, surprising herself. From the boys' wide-eyed and open-mouthed expressions, they were as surprised as she. Finally they laughed.

"You needed that," Joel softly said.

Was she that much of a grouch?

Joel didn't wait for her to respond, but looked into the engine. "The ignition coil has come loose. Let me plug it in." He did so, then hopped onto the seat and turned on the ignition. The tractor roared to life. He winked at her. "Let me pull this out of the barn before turning off the engine."

She nodded and shooed the boys out of the way. When she glanced at the porch where she'd put Cora down for her nap, April saw the little girl sit up and rub her eyes. When Joel drove out of the barn, Cora stood and started down the steps.

What was it about this cowboy that had all her children following him like a pied piper?

April scooped her daughter up before she could run in front of the tractor.

Joel parked beside the barn, where the plow's disc blades sat, and turned off the engine. He hopped out of the cab and waved at the boys.

Cora squirmed in her mother's arms.

"I'm impressed, but the real question is, will it start again?"

"Well, if it doesn't, we've got the wrench option."

"Thanks for getting it to work, but what are you doing out here?" She cringed at her abrupt words. *What a crab.*

"If you have a cup of coffee, I'd like to explain."

She studied him, but his gaze remained true, not shying away from her probing. Ross often wouldn't meet her gaze when he had a plan he knew she wouldn't approve of. "Okay."

Lots of questions flew through her mind as they walked inside. After a moment, it occurred to April how silent the boys were, which caused the hair at the back of her neck to stand up. April poured coffee for the adults and milk for the children, then joined the others at the table.

Surprisingly, Cora sat between her brothers on the bench seat on the other side of the table. The boys were wide-eyed and seemed to vibrate, waiting for—

April took a sip of coffee. That hair on the back of her neck felt as if it was dancing.

Wes looked at Joel, then his shoulders straightened and he seemed to grow up before her eyes, as if her son had given Joel permission. That didn't make sense.

Setting his mug on the table, Joel cleared his throat. "I've been hired by your sons to help you plant your fields this week."

That was not what she'd expected this rodeo cowboy to say. She turned to her sons.

"Todd and me wanted to get you some help after Mr. Moore's accident today, so when we saw Mr. Joel at the feed store, we talked it over and hired him to work this week," Wes explained.

"And we paid him, too. We gave him a dollar and thirty-seven cents." Todd's chest puffed out. "It's legal."

April groped with what she'd just heard. It had seemed to come out of nowhere. Staring at her mug, April considered her options, which were limited at best. The nightmare of Mr. Moore being knocked out this morning, landing on his right arm and dislocating it, sat in the forefront of her mind. Whom would she hire to replace him? Everybody else had their own ranches to care for, their own fields to plant. "You're not tied up this week at the rodeo?"

"I explained to the boys that I have morning chores that I need to do first, but I can be here before seven. That was fine with them."

She wanted to tell him no. She didn't need her boys getting any more involved with a traveling cowboy, but one look at her sons' precious faces and she knew she couldn't throw away their effort to help.

Todd worried his bottom lip and Wes reminded her of a cat waiting to catch a mouse. The thought of the boys going out and hiring Joel to help with the planting made her heart swell with pride. She knew she couldn't refuse.

"Then I guess you have a job."

The boys jumped with excitement. Cora didn't know what was happening, but she joined the celebration.

The grin on Joel's face made her fingers tingle, which scared her. Maybe she should back out now, before disaster struck. But as soon as the idea formed, she glanced at her sons. Could she crush their enthusiasm?

"Now, you'll need to tell me what you want done," Joel said, breaking into her internal debate.

"Don't worry," Wes piped in. "Mom's good at

telling people what to do." He said it so casually he didn't notice the smile on Joel's face or the wide-eyed look on his mother's.

"So these are the horses you picked up from the Landers ranch." Jack Murphy walked up to the corral housing the new stock.

When Joel returned earlier with Sadie and Helo, Jack had been in Amarillo. "Yup, these are the horses."

Jack rested his boot on the bottom rail. "They're a little young."

"True, but I think the lady needed the money."

Jack's brow wrinkled. "She say that?"

"Not exactly, but looking around, I could see things needed repair."

Jack rubbed his chin. "I worried about that when Vernon died. He talked to me when he was sick, asking me to keep buying from the Circle L Ranch. I agreed with him, wondering how his daughter-in-law could run that ranch by herself, having three little kids."

A perfect opening. "I guess that's why April's sons hired me to help this week."

"What?" Jack sounded as if he'd swallowed a frog.

"When I went to get the feed earlier, I saw the family. The boys slipped around the back while I was loading and hired me for the week. Apparently, their hired hand had an accident between the time I was there in the morning and when I saw them at the feed store in the afternoon."

"They hired you?" Jack asked.

"They did. I told them I'd have to finish chores here before I could go out to their place, but they were okay with the setup." Joel faced his boss straight on. "You okay with that?"

"Works for me. At least you'll have something to do with yourself instead of hanging around here, complaining you're bored."

"What? Was I that much of a problem?" Joel asked.

"Hank was afraid he was going to have to babysit you this week and didn't know what he was going to do. He's a cook, not a babysitter, and planned on telling you you needed to take up knitting."

"I couldn't have complained that much."

Jack's brow arched.

"Knitting?"

Both men grinned.

"How well did you know April's father-in-law?"

"April?" Jack's smile widened.

"Hey, a little background would help me understand what's going on and the situation there."

"Okay. We went back several years. Vernon loved the rodeo but loved his ranch more." Jack shook his head. "Kinda funny how his daughter-in-law took to ranching like a duck to water, but his son—

"Vernon said he never saw someone love ranching like April. She was a natural. There was nothing around the ranch she wouldn't do, or try to do, which surprised him.

"Too bad his son wanted nothing to do with the place. But Vernon and Grace never regretted Ross marrying April. They got the daughter they wanted and the grandbabies they'd hoped for."

Joel wanted to ask more, but he saw the gleam in Jack's eyes. "I asked if they were coming to the rodeo, but April—"

"April?" Jack again poked him, enjoying himself way too much.

"Mrs. Landers said no. Well, what she really said was 'we'll see,' which the boys knew was no. So I thought you could throw in tickets for both days of the rodeo. April's got a couple of budding cowboys there that need encouragement. If that's a problem, I'll pay for the tickets."

Jack's smile widened. "No, it's not a problem."

There was way too much satisfaction in Jack's answer.

"Yo, Jack, I need to talk to you," Graham "Shortie" McGraw shouted across the arena. "Now."

"Coming." Jack turned back to Joel. "See you later."

As Jack strode across the arena, Joel wondered

at his boss's reaction. What amusement did he find in Joel calling Mrs. Landers *April*? It was her name. Now, if he called her *sweetie* or *punkin* like his grandmother had called his grandfather, then Joel could've understood Jack's reaction. And why did giving away the tickets to the rodeo feel as though he'd made some deep commitment? They were tickets. That was all. So what had made Jack smile?

"He was way cool, Mom," Todd said, his spaghetti spilling out of his mouth. Sauce dotted his chin.

"Todd, keep your mouth closed while you're eating. It's polite."

Todd's fingers pushed the spaghetti back into his mouth. Wes snickered. She'd made the boys' favorite meal, hoping to take their minds off Joel Kaye.

After swallowing, Todd continued, "Did you see how Mr. Joel handled Helo and Sadie? He was so good, making friends with them first." He looked at his brother. "And Mr. Joel's birthday is in March and he's a real good cowboy."

Todd wasn't going to let go of his brother's false claims anytime soon.

Wes shrugged off the comment. "He was good with the lasso. I want to learn how to do that, too, 'cause you have to do that to be a cowboy. Opa was good. He started to show me how to throw, but—" Wes fell silent.

"Maybe Mr. Joel could show us," Todd suggested, his eyes going wide.

Wes perked up. "Yeah, that's a good idea. He threw as good as Opa."

Cora clapped her hands together, squishing a strand of spaghetti between them. "Yeah, cowboy."

The boys hadn't stopped talking about Joel since he'd left this afternoon. Of course, maybe that was a good sign, since the incident with Mr. Moore stepping on the pitchfork and knocking himself out had given them all a scare. Both boys had gone white, but Todd had seemed particularly shaken.

"I don't know if Mr. Joel will have the time to teach you. He'll be here to plant crops and do other chores that Mr. Moore would've done."

The boys fell silent, then traded calculating looks.

"Okay."

Why did Wes's *okay* worry her more than a protest?

April needed to stop any shenanigans before they got out of hand. "Maybe Mr. Waters could show you how to whirl a lariat after church sometime. He used to compete in the rodeo."

Todd rolled his eyes. "He's ancient, Mom. He must be fifty."

"No, eighty," Wes added.

Todd's brow crinkled. "Yeah, and I don't know if he would remember how to throw."

April choked on her spaghetti and quickly took a sip of tea. Andrew Waters was only thirty-eight.

"I don't know, boys. I don't want you to bother Mr. Joel while he's working."

The boys' faces fell.

"Aw, Mom." Wes put his fork down and frowned. He made it sound as if she'd just stomped on his dream.

Todd stared down at his plate, too, his posture only emphasizing how much the boys wanted Joel Kaye to teach them how to throw a lariat.

"I promise I'll check with Mr. Waters to see if he'll teach you how to throw." Her words went over like lead weights on a rubber raft.

"May I be excused?" Wes asked.

"Me, too," Todd added.

She felt lower than a snake's belly, stomping their hopes. She nodded and the boys slipped away from the table. Cora frowned, reaching for her brothers. April pulled Cora from her booster seat, wiped her hands and mouth, then set her on her feet. She hurried after her brothers.

"Good job, April," she murmured to herself. "No one's happy." And that included her.

April poured herself a large iced tea and wandered out onto the back porch. An hour and a half ago, she'd put three subdued children to bed, and those sad little faces had nearly brought her to her knees.

Scanning the bare fields behind the house, April felt a ray of hope and a huge helping of pride.

When Joel had told her the boys hired him, it'd taken her a moment to understand what he was saying. That her boys understood she needed help and wanted to provide it made her chest puff out with pride. It also disheartened her that they knew the ranch was in trouble.

With the death of her husband and in-laws over the past three years, she was now the only adult left on this ranch. Her neighbors had helped for a couple of months after Vernon's death, but they had their own ranches to care for. Lately, several of the ranchers at church had offered to rent her fields to plant their own cash crops.

She'd toyed with the idea, but it felt as though she'd be giving up on the ranch, on her dreams. She loved this place and had never thought that she'd be in this position.

Her father's job as a rig manager for a major oil company had kept them on the move throughout her life. She'd lived on several continents and in some exotic places, but none had felt like home until they moved to this place in the Texas Panhandle. When her father had been transferred to Lubbock her junior year in high school, she'd found her heart's desire on the Llano Estacado and the Caprock.

Added to the feeling of coming home, the first day in English class she'd met Ross Landers. He'd smiled at her and she'd been smitten. Ross had introduced her to all his friends, but it was when he brought her home to this ranch that she knew she was in love.

A home.

Roots.

And something that lasted. The Landers family had ranched this piece of land since the 1880s. Over five generations, through good times and bad, through times of plenty and drought, the family had persevered. That legacy flooded her with purpose and direction. She could do this. Needed to do this.

April and Ross had married a week after graduating from high school and he'd immediately gone to work on a rig out in West Texas, which had surprised her, since Ross had never mentioned he didn't want to stay on the ranch. He visited home often while she was pregnant with Wes but missed the baby's birth. Two years later, when she got pregnant with Todd, Ross immediately got one of the treasured jobs as a roughneck on an oil platform in the Gulf of Mexico that her father oversaw. His excuse for taking that job had been that the extra money he'd receive would help with the expenses of the new baby.

Ross never came back for any length of time after he left. He made it home sporadically for the next four years. When his mother, Grace, was diagnosed with breast cancer, Ross came home that Christmas. That gave April hope that he'd changed, but she quickly learned that wasn't the case. Ross refused to take his mom to any of her chemo sessions. He did promise to attend Wes's first-grade Christmas pageant, but he didn't show. Instead he got drunk with other oil field workers from West Texas. With Todd, Ross would either throw the four-year-old around as if he was a rag doll, hold him upside down by his feet or ignore him, which confused the boy.

When Ross took the assignment on a new rig in the Gulf, Vernon, Grace and April all breathed a sigh of relief that his disruptive presence was gone. Six weeks later Ross died in a freak accident. After they buried him, April discovered she was pregnant with Cora. The money she'd received from Ross's life insurance, which her in-laws insisted she save and use for her babies, was now almost gone.

Her father-in-law had had to borrow against the ranch to help finish paying for Grace's care and meds in the last months of her life. She'd died a year ago Christmas. Vernon died the following September. Now April had to come up with a plan to pay off the loan or lose the ranch. Would the money she made on the sunflowers and hay be enough? Did she need to rent out the other fields on the ranch?

She turned her eyes to the fallow field. Would she survive?

"Lord, I know You have the answers to this problem, but—"

"Mom, what are you doing out here?"

She looked up and saw Todd standing by the back door in his superhero pajamas, his feet bare.

"Thinking. Praying."

"Are you mad we hired Mr. Joel? He can do Mr. Moore's job since he got hurt."

"No, I'm not mad. I'm proud of you and your brother for thinking about the ranch. Opa would be pleased, too." Her solution to the problem wouldn't have been to hire Joel, but she couldn't ignore her sons' solution. It still amazed her that Joel agreed to the deal for a dollar thirty-seven. *Why'd he do it?*

A grin curved Todd's mouth. "I'll help Mr. Joel. So will Wes."

"I know you will."

"But I'm kinda worried about Sadie and Helo. Are they scared being in a new place?"

"You'll have to ask Mr. Joel tomorrow how they're doing. He'll know."

Todd thought about it, nodded and tore down the hall to his bedroom.

Watching her younger son disappear into his room, she knew her boys would keep her on her toes with creative thinking all through school. Teenage years promised to be…a challenge.

She retrieved her tea off the porch rail. Wouldn't Vernon and Grace be proud of their grandsons? She knew they would.

Would their father?

Joel lingered over his coffee, the empty plate that had held his barbecue sitting before him. Working with Jack Murphy doing whatever needed to be done around the rodeo helped defray his expenses on the road and kept him busy. What had he done when he was eighteen, traveling with the rodeo, and had the day off? Shoot the breeze with the other young cowboys or brag about his latest score in the different rodeo events? Of course, things hadn't changed since he was eighteen. Cowboys still bragged about how good they were and how they would capture the ultimate prize of the championship belt buckle given to the number one cowboy in the Professional Rodeo Cowboys Association, or PRCA.

"You need a refill on that coffee?" Hank Calder asked. Hank ran the concessions for the rodeo. He also cooked for the rodeo workers. If any cowboy wanted a meal, they could buy it. Of course, meals were included with the deal Joel had struck with Jack and his boss, Steve Carter.

"Sure."

Hank topped off the coffee and sat opposite Joel at the picnic table.

"So, how's it going? You enjoying this vagabond life?" Hank grinned. The instant Joel joined the rodeo, he and Hank had struck up a friendship.

"I was just thinking about that. When you're young and green, the traveling and excitement of being in a different city every week is appealing." He shrugged. "Then you grow up."

Hank grinned. "I hear ya. I've got aches and pains in places I didn't know existed. And I find new ones every day."

Joel couldn't help but smile. "You got that right. I've worked beside my dad and gramps since I could sit in a saddle and didn't experience these aches and pains." He fell silent. "I didn't feel old when I put in an eighteen-hour day at the ranch. What happened?"

"When you get bucked off a horse or bull, it feels like you've been run over by a truck, which is different than a hard day's work on a ranch."

"You're right."

"So why'd you come back on the circuit?"

Good question. "Circumstances. My sister recently married and I wanted the newlyweds to have some time together on the family ranch." Of course, Gramps was still there. "Too many bosses. She married Caleb Jensen."

"It was your sister he married?"

"Yup. She came home and helped put together that charity rodeo that helped all the ranchers west of Fort Worth. She and Caleb got to know each other, and—" He shrugged.

"He was a mighty good pickup man, but I understand how the rodeo can wear out a man."

"I wanted to see if rodeo life was as much fun as it had been at eighteen."

"And?"

"I'm still checking it out. But the longer I go and the more points I get, the ache becomes secondary."

Hank chuckled and walked back into the kitchen.

After cleaning up his dinner plate, Joel visited Helo and Sadie. He wanted to be prepared in case April's boys asked about their horses. The new horses recognized him and came to the edge of the corral. Sadie bumped him with her nuzzle.

"Sorry, girl, I didn't bring you anything. I just wanted to check on you so I can answer the questions I know I'll get."

Smiling, Joel thought about those little boys who'd barged into his life and thrown him a curve he hadn't seen coming. It was just supposed to have been a run-of-the-mill rodeo run to pick up horses. Instead, he'd run headlong into a situation that laid him out flat. As ridiculous as it sounded, he welcomed the job offer. For the balance of the week, he'd be ranching and helping

April, a woman who managed to yank his heart in a way it hadn't been yanked before.

It was the Western thing to do to help someone in distress. It was also the Christian thing to do.

He could help her this week, but...

Sadie poked her muzzle in his face again.

He held up his hands. "I promise you, I don't have a thing." He stroked her neck. The horse nuzzled his hands, then dipped her head toward his pockets. Discovering no apples or carrots, she turned and joined the other horses in the corral.

"Not interested in me. Just wanted a treat?"

Jack stopped beside him.

"It looks like I'm losing my touch with the females," Joel grumbled, nodding to Sadie.

"I doubt it."

"Don't see any ladies lining up beside my trailer."

"That's 'cause you have a not-interested sign written all over you that even the other cowboys can read."

Joel opened his mouth to argue, then swallowed his words.

"Good, you're not going to deny it."

"I'm here to compete." What Joel wanted was a championship belt buckle and to finish out a dream. Nothing more.

Jack rubbed his chin. "You sure it was the boys who hired you and you just didn't volunteer?"

The question took Joel by surprise. "No, I didn't volunteer. Why would you ask that?"

Jack shook his head. "You've been restless lately."

"What are you talking about? I've been doing great in my events and gaining points."

"True, but there's something—"

"You sound like my sister, trying to look into my head and tell me what I'm thinking, and she's going through training to become a counselor."

Jack raised his hands in surrender. "Forget it. I didn't mean to step in that snake pit."

What on earth was Jack talking about? He was on course for winning that championship belt buckle.

"How old are those boys?"

"Six and eight."

"I'd like to meet those entrepreneurs. If you have time, bring them by the rodeo this week." Jack started toward his trailer.

"Not a problem. Once I mention it to them, wild horses wouldn't keep them away."

The question was, would their mother go for it? He didn't know, but he hoped she would. Maybe it would help April relax and open up. He found he wanted to know more about this woman.

Chapter Three

Joel felt as awkward as a high-school freshman with his first crush as he drove to the Landers ranch. Before he could get out of his vehicle, the boys scrambled down the porch stairs and raced toward him.

The screen door slammed. April, along with Cora, stood on the porch. "Have you eaten yet?"

"No, just grabbed a cup of coffee before I did chores."

"Well, I've got eggs, bacon, hash browns and biscuits. And lots of coffee."

His mouth watered. "Your stock fed?"

"I got it."

"I helped," Todd proudly announced.

Joel smiled at the boy. "And I know your help made things easier for your mom."

Wes didn't speak up, but Joel knew he wasn't going to let his younger brother outdo him. Joel winked at Wes, acknowledging him.

The smell of bacon and eggs drifted out the screen door, making Joel's stomach rumble, which was heard by all. "Then let's feed the workers so we can get this day rolling."

Laughing, Todd raced inside, Joel following.

Wes and Cora were already seated. Todd pulled out a chair.

"Wash your hands, young man."

"Aw, Mom."

"I need to wash my hands, too." Joel held out his hands.

"'Kay. Follow me."

Todd led Joel through the living room to the hall beyond. The first door stood open and Todd walked in. He stepped up onto the stool and turned on the water.

"Mom's strict about washing our hands." He grabbed the soap, lathered up and passed the bar to Joel.

"I know. My mom was the same," Joel whispered, bending close. "And I had to have an inspection. But you know what was worse?"

Todd's eyes widened. "What?"

"My grandmother. She wouldn't allow a speck of dirt. I've been sent back to the bathroom many times. One time I had dirt here—" he pointed to a spot on the back of his hand close to the wrist bone "—and she made me go back and wash again. I got a second inspection."

Todd thought about it. "Mom's not that hard."

Once finished, they joined the others at the table.

"Wes, would you like to pray?" April asked.

During the prayer, Joel heard a noise and opened one eye to see Cora grab a piece of bacon. April frowned. She noticed him, and they traded smiles. Adults holding down the fort.

"Amen."

April dished eggs for Cora and Todd. Wes helped himself to a biscuit and hash browns. After serving himself a generous helping of eggs and hash browns, Joel dug into the meal. Watching the children eat, Joel flashed back to the scenes of his youth around the dinner table. Seeing April interact with her children made him keenly aware of how alone he was. One day in the future, he'd like to have a family of his own, which oddly resembled the people at this table.

Todd put down his knife. The biscuit on his plate sported a layer of butter, topped with peach preserves. "Why are you smiling, Mr. Joel?"

"I was remembering when I was your age and eating with my parents and grandparents."

"Wow, you can remember that long ago?" Todd murmured in awe.

April choked on her coffee. Wes snickered.

"Of course I do even if my sister has her doubts."

"I mean, where are your mom and dad?"

"They're in Heaven now."

"Oh." Todd stared down at his plate, his shoulders hunched. "My dad and Oma and Opa are in Heaven, too."

The smile on April's face disappeared.

"Do you miss them?" Todd whispered, a catch in his voice.

The ache in the little boy's voice touched Joel. He also knew Wes waited for his answer.

"I do. They went to Heaven many years ago, but sometimes I see a sunset or a flower and it reminds me of my mom and grandma. Now, with my dad, if I see a horse the same color as his, I think he would like that horse."

"Oh." Todd thought over the answer. "Are you still sad?"

April bit her lip, waiting.

He hadn't expected a counseling session at breakfast and wondered what his sister, the counselor in training, would tell him to say.

Lord, I need some words of wisdom. "I was sad when it happened, but now I can remember them and smile. I recall the good and funny things, like when my dad stepped in a bucket of water I left beside the back door. Or the time my mom got mad at me and threw an egg. I ducked and it hit my sister, who was coming into the kitchen." He winked at the boys. "You should've seen her face with all the yolk and egg white running down her cheeks and dripping off her chin. My mom's reaction, her expression—" he dropped his jaw and let his eyes go wide to demonstrate the reaction "—was funnier than my sister's."

The boys laughed and he caught April smiling.

"I did my share of things that my mom got on me about."

"What?" the boys asked.

Joel glanced at April. "I do need to keep a few secrets."

"Aw," the boys groaned.

"You better eat while your eggs are still warm," April warned.

Reluctantly, Wes and Todd started eating, but they constantly looked at Joel, as though they were afraid he'd vanish into thin air if they didn't look at him every few minutes.

April watched the boys wolf down their breakfast, but what broke her heart was their constant checking to make sure Joel didn't disappear. Would this be a bigger disaster than she feared?

Her fields would be planted, but at what cost?

Wes and Todd slipped from their seats and headed for the back door.

"Put your dishes by the sink," April instructed.

"Aw, Mom," Wes complained, but obeyed.

Todd opened his mouth to voice his objection, but with one look at her, he swallowed the gripe and slipped his plate beside his brother's.

"Down," Cora asked.

Joel took the little girl out of her booster chair

and placed her on her feet. She followed her brothers outside.

They were alone in the kitchen, finishing their coffee. The warm, intimate feeling of them together, lingering over breakfast, discussing the ranch, rattled her. She wanted to see Joel as nothing but a hired hand, but somehow her brain and heart went mushy.

She held up her cup. "More?"

"Sure. Top me off."

She grabbed the coffee carafe and refilled both cups. Sitting down, she took a deep breath to steady herself.

"So tell me what you've decided to plant and what fields you plan to use." Joel took a sip of his coffee.

His question jerked her back to the present. Most of the night she'd prayed and wrestled with what to do on the ranch—as well as fantasies about this tall, toe-tingling cowboy. Early this morning she'd come to a decision. "I want to plant hay in the north field, and in the west field I thought I'd go with your suggestion and plant sunflowers."

They traded glances, and April thought she saw him smile, but it was gone so quickly that maybe she'd been wishing it.

"I think you made a good choice. So where are these fields?"

"Let's go take a drive and I'll show you."

They all piled into April's truck, Cora and Todd in the backseat, Wes between April and Joel. She drove out to the north field first, pointing out the section that needed to be planted with hay.

"At mile marker 123 is the start of the field," she explained and continued to drive.

"Right there by the sign for the feed store is where our field ends." Wes pointed, his arm shooting out and nearly catching Joel on the chin.

She glanced at Wes. "I didn't know you knew the boundaries."

"Yeah, Opa showed me," he answered casually without looking at her.

Words piled up in her throat, and she couldn't spit one out.

Within twenty minutes, April finished showing Joel the other field she wanted to plant.

"And the rest of the fields, I'll rent out. I've had a couple of the folks at church offer to rent a field."

"Good idea."

April nodded. "If something's not in that field, I could lose topsoil, and that I can't afford to do."

"Opa always talked to us about the ranch," Wes said. "And how to care for it."

Her son knew more than she credited him with. Vernon had been a great teacher.

"I see your grandfather taught you well."

Wes sat up straighter. "Opa told me I needed

to plant a field and not let it lay fallow, 'cause you don't want to lose the topsoil. We are stewards of this land."

Vernon had always said that. April felt pride her son had picked up his grandfather's attitude and ashamed she hadn't realized her son's connection to the land. The boys hiring Joel should've sent her a clue.

"When harvest time comes around, whoever harvests the fields you rent out might do yours, too."

His words, like a slap in the face, reminded her that he wouldn't be here in the fall to harvest the crops, but they told her he knew his way around a ranch.

The boys chatted with Joel while she drove back to the house. The instant she stopped the truck by the kitchen door, Joel slipped out and walked to the tractor. "So let's pray that your tractor will start this morning," Joel said, "or I'll be using that wrench. Where's the key?"

"Inside the kitchen door."

The children stood by the truck and watched him retrieve the key, start the tractor and attach the blades to the back of it.

"I'll do the hay field first, then go to the west field and plow and plant the sunflowers today. I'll replow the hay field tomorrow and plant it."

When his words finally registered, April's gaze jerked to his. The man knew what to do and didn't need her instruction or prodding. Such a simple gesture softened her heart. "Sounds good."

He climbed down from the seat and walked toward her. "I'll give you my cell number in case you need to contact me."

April held up her hand, reached inside the truck and grabbed the pad and pencil she kept in the center console. "I'm ready."

He rattled off his cell-phone number.

"I guess you should have the house number, just in case, as you said." The corner of his mouth kicked up, making her stomach dance.

He whipped out his phone from the front pocket of his Western shirt and entered the number as she said it.

Once he had the number saved, he waved the boys to his side. "Okay, let's do rock, paper, scissors to see who rides with me out to the north field. When I do the west field, the other boy will go."

"Aren't they a little young to be riding in the cab?" April asked.

"You're never too young to learn how to use a tractor. My dad had me ride with him when I was Todd's age, and I was plowing fields after I turned ten."

"Opa let me ride with him, Mom," Wes hastily added.

If the man had used any other argument, she

would've shot down the idea, but the boys needed to know how to operate the machinery and how to plow if they were going to maintain the ranch. She knew Vernon had been teaching the boys, but hearing them repeat the lessons would've made him proud. It certainly made her smile. After surveying three waiting males, she said, "All right."

The boys pounded their little fists on their hands. April stood rooted to the spot, watching.

"One. Two. Three."

The boys went along and Todd won.

"Can we try again?" Wes asked.

Joel put his hand on Wes's shoulder. "You're with me to plant the sunflowers."

Wes looked up at Joel, than at his brother. "Okay." He didn't argue or pout, but trusted Joel enough to go along with his turn being second.

April worked hard not to let her jaw drop that her son offered no argument.

"I guess Wes can help me get my vegetable garden ready to plant."

"And Mr. Joel told me some stuff to do around here," Wes added.

"Those chores can wait until you help your mom plant the garden."

Wes nodded.

They watched as Joel drove the tractor to the north section of land.

Cora looked back at April. "I go, too."

"We'll work right here and plant some of your favorite vegetables."

"Cupcakes?"

Wes snickered. "That's not a vegetable. Carrots, peas, potatoes—those are vegetables."

Cora folded her arms over her chest and pursed her lips.

"You like giving Sammie a carrot, don't you?" Wes asked.

"And you like mashed potatoes?" April added, knowing it was Cora's favorite food.

Cora nodded.

"Well, we'll plant potatoes and strawberries and watch them grow." Throwing in the strawberries clinched the deal. Both children agreed to work in the garden.

April turned off the computer, finished with her accounts. She melted into her chair and took a deep breath. Relief washed over her, making her light-headed.

"Thank You, Lord."

The roller-coaster events of the past couple of days still had her reeling. By dinner tonight, the sunflowers were planted, along with her garden, and she had three happy, satisfied children. Tomorrow the hay field would be done. There was hope.

Hope.

Such a small word, with some giant results.

Despite her offer, Joel didn't stay for dinner, but the boys beamed with pride as they told her how they'd helped Mr. Joel. She hadn't seen Wes and Todd that excited about anything since before their grandfather died.

Intrigued by the story Joel had told about his parents and his grandmother at breakfast, she felt there was something more to the story than he told. She'd like to know what he'd left out.

"Stop," she chided herself. Joel would only be here the balance of the week. The man's presence had managed to scramble the brains of all members of the family, herself included. That should be a warning, flashing bright, telling her of danger. And yet, she found herself ignoring those caution lights.

If she thought about it, Joel's attitude differed as much from Ross's as night from day. Joel welcomed her boys, piercing the shield she'd built around her heart in a way she couldn't stop. When news of Ross's death had reached April, she'd grieved with his parents, but she'd felt guilty that she wasn't devastated. She had two little boys to take care of. When she discovered she was pregnant again, she didn't have any time to grieve—at least, that was what she told herself. Was that simply an excuse?

The phone rang. Instantly, April picked it up, since she didn't want the ring to wake any of the kids. "Hello."

"April, honey, how are you doing and how are the kids?"

"Hi, Mom. We're all doing well. Are you and Dad going to be coming to spend Easter with us this year?" Her mother lived in Houston, the closest big city to the platform her father managed. The children were excited about seeing their grandparents.

"Uh, that's what I'm calling about. Your father has a new assignment. They want him to manage one of the new drilling platforms off Brazil. He's leaving tomorrow. I'm going to put the house here on the market by the end of the week, then look for a house for us in Rio de Janeiro."

"How long is his assignment?"

"At least two years, maybe three. They think this area is a gold mine, which means we might be there longer. I'm going to have to learn to speak Portuguese." She spoke Bahasa Indonesian and Dutch, which she'd learned while they were in Indonesia. And when they were in Ghana her mother had learned Dagbanli, but she couldn't remember any of April's friends' names. She'd even forgotten April's twelfth birthday because she'd been too busy managing a reception in honor of the president of Ghana given by the oil company.

April's stomach sank. "So we won't see you this Easter. Maybe Christmas?"

"I don't know. Things are still hectic. I want

to see those babies of yours, but this move just caught us off guard. Your dad was offered a very nice bonus to take this job."

A familiar refrain that her father had accepted this new challenge didn't shock her. His job always was number one. April had realized it the Christmas she was eight and her father couldn't make it off the oil platform. He'd come home the week of New Year's and explained that his working on Christmas meant he could buy her a nicer bicycle as a gift. What she wanted was her father sharing Christmas with his family.

"I know the kids will be disappointed not to see their grandparents. They are growing so quickly that you won't recognize them."

"I'm disappointed not to be able to see them, too, but this opportunity just showed up and we couldn't turn it down."

Nothing had changed with her parents. Living with her in-laws had taught her to expect more, but then she had to realize she was talking to her mom.

"You know, maybe you and the kids could come to Brazil and spend Christmas with us. It would be such a treat for them to be in the warm weather."

Instead of enduring the cold wind and weather in the Panhandle. April heard her mother's implication although no words were spoken.

"I don't know, Mom. Who would take care of the animals and ranch while we were gone?"

The line remained quiet for several moments. Finally, her mother said, "Your dad and I have talked about it. Both your husband and his family are dead, and all you have are those precious children. We think you should consider selling the ranch and moving to the city. Without the burden of that place, you could have time for your children. Find a job you like or go back to school and get a degree. You can't do all that ranch work by yourself."

Her mother's words felt like a knife in her heart. Sure, there were problems, but she wasn't going to sell her children's inheritance no matter what. Vernon had bragged how big the ranch had been in the early 1900s, when the Landerses had a big family and relatives who lived close by. But slowly, the family members had died or moved away. Vernon and Grace had only had one son instead of the seven that Vernon's parents had had. The Circle L Ranch might not be the size it once was, but she wasn't going to sell or desert it. It was part of her heart.

April knew her father wanted her to sell the ranch, but she'd thought she had her mother's support. Apparently not. "Thanks for the input, Mom. I'll think about it."

"I know you love that place, but face reality. It's a mighty big job and there's only you."

"I have help to plant this year." The words were out before she thought.

"Oh?"

It was the truth even if Joel was only here for the week. "I know the kids will miss seeing you. You and Dad might want to call them before Dad leaves and explain your exciting news."

"We'll try."

In other words, it won't happen. "I pray things will go smoothly with the move, Mom."

"We can talk with the kids over the computer and they can see our new house once we're settled."

April's heart broke. "They'll love it."

"I know you're disappointed, sweetheart. I'm sorry."

The familiar refrain rang hollow. "I know."

When she hung up, April's mind raced over all the birthdays, holidays and graduations her father had missed. She didn't want that for her children. She wanted her kids to have a connection with their home and good memories of growing up—memories like going to the rodeo every year and having a tall cowboy show them how to lasso a horse or a cow.

Determination filled her heart. She wouldn't fail her babies. "Thank you, Lord, for sending help to plant my field, but I'm going to need a long-range plan and a way to make this happen."

And did that long-range plan own cowboy boots?

Chapter Four

The following day, Joel finished planting the hay field well before 10:00 a.m. Next they tackled the chores around the barn. Finally, Joel roped Buckwheat and Sammie and tied them to the posts outside the barn.

"What are we doing, Mr. Joel?" Wes asked.

The screen door slammed and April and Cora appeared.

"If you're going to own a horse, you're going to need to learn to groom him. Had your opa shown you how to do that?"

"He did, but Todd might need to be shown again."

Joel heard a choked laugh. He didn't look at April because he knew he'd laugh, too.

"Then we'll do that."

With a couple of buckets of soapy water, a wooden step stool he found in the barn and

Buckwheat and Sammie tied up, Joel gave a sponge to each boy.

"Is this just a boy party or can the girls help?"

The boys glanced at Joel.

"Of course. I know Cora's going to need to learn this, too." Joel motioned them forward. "Mom, you might want to keep Miss Cora toward the front of Sammie."

They began to wash both horses, with Joel adding commentary on what to do. He held Cora up so she could run the sudsy sponge over Sammie's back. "Let's rinse off Sammie and Buckwheat."

Wes picked up the hose and sprayed Buckwheat. When he handed the hose to his brother, Todd accidentally sprayed Joel in the face.

"Oh." Todd's face went white.

Everyone froze, unsure of Joel's reaction. Even the horses stilled. Joel threw back his head and laughed. He snatched the hose and spritzed Todd. When April started to object, he aimed the water dead center at her chest. She looked down at the wet spot, lunged for the hose and got a face full of water. The water fight was on.

Twenty minutes later everyone was soaked. Joel turned off the hose. He hadn't had a water fight since he was in the fifth grade.

Water fell off him in rivulets.

April looked at him, then snorted, drawing the boys' attention.

Todd laughed first, followed by Wes, Cora, Joel and April.

The horses shook, sending more water flying, bringing another round of laughs.

April handed out towels, drying the kids before she wiped down Sammie. Joel took care of Buckwheat.

The laughter died when a truck drove up and Beth Moore opened the driver's door. She observed the dripping kids and adults. "A water fight?"

"We wash horseys." Cora pointed at Wes. "Brother sprayed Mr. Joel. Mr. Joel sprayed brother and Mama." She giggled. "Me, too."

The truck's passenger door opened and a man in his early fifties slid out. His right arm was in a sling and he sported a goose egg on the right side of his forehead.

The children fell silent.

"How are you feeling today, Albert?" April walked to the truck.

"I'm doing fine, but Beth and I were worried how you'd get your fields planted."

Joel saw April blush as drops of water continued to drip off her shirt.

"The boys hired Joel for this week. He's with the rodeo, and he's helping us plant the fields and taking care of some chores."

Beth surveyed the group. "I see," she said, but laughter colored her words.

"Joel gave the kids instructions on how to bathe their horses, but things got a little out of hand." She shrugged. "And a little foolish."

Al remained quiet, but his gaze missed nothing.

"Well, we were concerned and planned to call the church to get volunteers to come out and help you, but it looks like you have things under control," Beth explained.

Water continued to drip off Joel, drawing the couple's attention. Joel tried to keep his smile casual to cover his awkwardness. Nothing like standing in the middle of the yard dripping wet and laughing to make folks think you were nuts.

Beth leaned close and whispered to April. She drew back, her eyes wide.

"You be sure to call the church secretary and tell her what you're bringing for Sunday's lunch on the ground." Beth opened the driver's door and slipped in.

"I'll do that." April stepped toward Al. "How are you doing?"

"He's milking this for all it's worth," Beth answered before Al opened his mouth, "that's how he's doing." She started the truck. "C'mon, old man. You need your nap."

April closed the passenger door for Al. "I wish that accident never happened. You be sure and let me know when you get the bill. I want to pay for it."

Al rested his hand on April's. "I know you will, but God sees needs and sends miracles."

Frowning, April stepped back and watched the truck drive away.

She turned to Joel. "Let's finish with the horses, then I think we all need a change of clothes."

"Mr. Joel doesn't have any dry clothes," Wes pointed out.

"Not to worry. Once y'all are dried, the wind should've taken care of me. 'Sides, I won't melt."

The boys gave him a puzzled look. "Why would you melt?" Todd asked.

"Your mom can explain it later."

After drying the horses, Joel walked them to the corral, while April took the children inside.

Leaning against the fence, Joel thought of the water fight. It did his soul good to laugh and play. He hadn't been that foolish since he was a teen. But he knew it helped April and her children more than it did him or the horses. The expression on her face when she got smacked with the stream of water had been priceless. It had taken her several moments to understand he was playing, as if she couldn't recall how to do it. But once she keyed in to the play, she'd embraced the fun. Too bad the older couple had showed up and robbed the situation of all its pleasure.

He felt a nuzzle by his right ear. He glanced over his shoulder, reached up and rubbed Sammie's neck. "You looking for a treat? Not happy with just a bath but want a reward, too?"

The horse nodded.

"Well, I can't go inside and drip all over April's kitchen floor."

The screen door slamming brought his attention to the house. Todd stood outside, his face grim.

"Your horse wants a carrot. Would you like to get him one?"

Todd nodded and disappeared into the kitchen only to reemerge moments later with a carrot. Walking to the fence, he handed Joel the treat.

"Don't you want to give it to Sammie yourself?"

"No." He walked to the side of the barn and sat on the ground, his back against the wooden siding. It looked as if the weight of the world sat on those small shoulders, which tugged at Joel's heart. What had happened that changed Todd's attitude from laughing and playful to down and troubled?

Joel searched his mind. The only thing he could think of was the Moores driving up. The boys had mentioned that their mother's help had been hurt, but was there something else there?

Casually, Joel walked to where Todd sat. The boy didn't look up or acknowledge him in any way. Settling by Todd, Joel leaned back against the barn, his knees raised. He rested his forearm on his knees, knowing he couldn't push this youngster any more than he could've rushed Sadie and Helo a couple days ago.

In the corral before them, Joel watched the two horses. "I think Buckwheat and Sammie enjoyed their bath. I know the rest of us did. Didn't you?"

Todd found the dirt by his small boot extremely interesting. "Yeah."

So much for a light conversation. Apparently, Todd wasn't going to make this easy. He needed to rope this problem from a different direction. "Is this your favorite place to think?"

Todd shrugged.

"When I was growing up, I had a place in our barn, in the hayloft. It was a good thinking place. I sometimes went there when I did something I knew would get me in trouble.

"One time, my mom had made a birthday cake for my grandmother. Chocolate with Gran's special icing." He paused and made an appreciative sound. "I tried to sneak a big finger full of icing off the cake, but instead I pushed the cake off the counter. It made such a terrible sound when it hit the floor and the plate shattered into a million pieces, with cake and icing exploding all over the kitchen." It had been a spectacular mess.

Todd looked at him.

"I can't tell you how scared I was. I ran out

into the barn and hid. Of course, my sister ratted me out."

"But you didn't hurt your grandmother." Todd's voice quivered with emotion.

Joel's heart ached. "True, but we had no cake that birthday."

Todd hugged his knees and rested his head against his thighs.

"What happened, Todd?"

Tears rolled down the boy's cheeks. "After you picked up Sadie and Helo, Mr. Moore came to work. He got the pitchfork down, but Mom called him up to the house. I wanted to help, so I got the fork and tried to put straw in Sammie's stall. Wes walked into the barn and saw me. He said he'd tell on me for messing with the pitchfork. I got scared and put it against the stall wall and left the barn." He shrugged. "I guess it fell down and that's how Mr. Moore stepped on it. It was my fault."

It was, but this little boy didn't need that rebuke. "Do you see why you were told not to mess with the pitchfork?"

He nodded and with the back of his sleeve wiped the tears from his face.

"I understand that you never would've wanted Mr. Moore to get hurt."

"I didn't want that" came the wobbly reply.

"I didn't mean to ruin my grandma's cake, either. We have to fess up when we do wrong.

Gran and Ma forgave me, but my sister wasn't as nice and reminded me of it often."

Todd glanced up at him. "Girls are like that."

"True." Joel heard a movement and glanced over his shoulder. April stood at the corner of the barn. Todd didn't notice.

"I think you need to tell your mom what happened. You'll feel better."

Todd stared at his hands. "Really? We can't just keep it a secret between us?"

"I think it's best if you tell your mom."

Taking a deep breath, Todd thought a moment. "'Kay." He stood and waited for Joel to stand. "Let's go."

Todd marched to the house, much like a condemned man to the gallows.

Admiration filled Joel's heart for this little cowboy.

April finished putting sandwiches on the table when Joel and Todd walked into the kitchen. When she'd gone out earlier to look for the boys, she'd overheard Joel and Todd talking. She'd quietly backed away and rushed inside the house. The last thing she heard was "Tell your mom."

"Lunch is just sandwiches and cookies, but I'm told I make a mean sandwich."

"I'd like that." Joel nodded toward Todd.

Thanks, she mouthed.

After the blessing, the kids dug into their lunch.

Todd reached for his sandwich but rested his hands by his plate.

"Todd, aren't you hungry?"

He shook his head.

April leaned close and whispered, "Do you need to talk to me?"

He nodded.

"Joel, would you watch things for a few minutes?"

"Sure."

Todd slipped from his chair and headed toward the office.

April followed.

"What's happening?" Wes asked.

April didn't hear Joel's explanation, but followed her son into the office.

"I got to tell you something," Todd began.

April closed the door and sat in her chair. "What do you need to tell me?"

Todd's lips quivered. "It's my fault that Mr. Moore got hurt."

"Oh."

"I know I wasn't supposed to touch it, but I wanted to help Mr. Moore feed the horses, so when you called him, I picked up the pitchfork and tried to move the hay to help. It was heavy." He stopped and took a breath. "Wes saw me and ran out of the barn. I got scared and left the pitchfork against the stalls and ran out. It must've fallen and Mr. Moore stepped on it."

He spoke the last words so softly that April had to lean forward to hear. She sat back and looked at her son.

"I'm sorry, Mom. Mr. Joel told me I needed to tell you. I didn't mean for Mr. Moore to get hurt, but—" He looked up at her, his fear and sorrow clear in his eyes.

"But he did," April softly finished.

His bottom lip quivered.

"We have rules to help us be safe, and that's why I expect you to obey them."

His shoulders hunched.

April wished her husband had learned to follow the safety rules on the oil rig. Maybe he would be alive today.

"Do you promise me you'll follow the rules from now on?"

He nodded his head.

She wrapped her arms around her precious little boy and hugged him.

Lord, how am I going to raise them?

Todd started to squirm. She released him, trying to keep the tears out of her own eyes.

"I'm hungry, Mom."

April didn't know whether to laugh or cry. "Then let's go eat."

When they walked into the kitchen, the others at the table stopped eating.

"Is everything okay?" Joel asked.

"Yes."

"Mom," Wes said, "while you were gone, I asked Mr. Joel how Sadie and Helo were doing. Could we go see them?"

Todd perked up.

The request took April by surprise. She looked around the table and three little eager faces stared back at her. The fields were planted and the fun time they'd had grooming Buckwheat and Sammie seemed to have revitalized the kids. It had been a hard time since Vernon's death. They could use a little break. Besides, she hadn't picked up her money.

"Okay. We can visit and see the horses, then I need to go by the grocery store."

A cheer went up.

"But I'll need to run some errands, so we can't stay all afternoon."

Todd smiled up at her. "Thanks, Mom."

Glancing up, she caught Joel's smile, which did funny things to her stomach. Maybe this trip to the rodeo wasn't a good idea. But the children's excitement drowned out her doubts.

Joel parked his truck by the other trailers behind the coliseum, and April stopped hers beside his. He helped the kids out and they walked into the building.

A temporary corral housing the horses stood in the back of the coliseum by a large set of double doors leading to the outside. A smaller door by the double doors was how most of the cowboys went in and out after the initial conversion of the coliseum into a rodeo arena.

"There they are." Joel pointed toward the horses.

That was all it took for the boys to break into a run.

"Be careful," April called out, hurrying behind the boys as fast as Cora's little legs could follow. April didn't let go of her daughter's hand.

The horses moved restlessly around the corral and after a few moments, Wes pointed. "There's Sadie. She's by that brown horse and they're eating." Wes looked over his shoulder. "They look okay, Mom."

"And Helo is beside her." Todd stood on his left foot with his right foot propped on top of it. "I think they've made some friends."

Standing behind the boys, Joel slipped his hands into the back pockets of his jeans. "They seem a good fit with the stock we have."

April came to a stop beside Joel. She looked at the horses she sold to the rodeo, but her mind went to the man standing next to her. The sturdiness of him reassured her. It wouldn't be hard to rely on him. She shied away from the thought and stepped back. She wouldn't rely on a traveling man.

"They've been getting along with the other horses, no problem," Joel added.

She swallowed hard. "Good."

The boys turned toward him.

"I'm glad. When I started first grade, it was nice to know some kids in my class. They went to our church." Todd looked back into the corral. "I'm glad they're happy."

Cora pulled her hand free from April's and ran toward her brothers and the horses. April's heart stopped. Cora was short enough to slide under the lowest bar of the corral and charge straight into the animals.

April lurched forward, but Joel stepped in front of Cora and swept her into his arms, lifting her to his shoulder. Cora screamed with delight.

Still shaking from her daughter's antics, April stopped and took a deep breath. "Cora Marie, come here."

The tone of April's voice cut through her daughter's giggles.

Cora stilled.

"Please put her down," April directed. Her tone brooked no defiance.

Joel complied.

April moved to stand in front of her daughter and squatted down. "That was naughty of you. You will hold my hand and behave yourself or I will take you home."

The boys' eyes widened. "Mom," they said together.

April stood. "You both know if Cora had run

into that corral she could've been hurt. She needs to pay attention around stock just like you boys do, and not because I want to be mean, but because I want her to be safe."

The boys didn't protest.

Wes came to Cora's side. "I'll help you hold her hand."

Tears stung April's eyes at Wes's thoughtfulness.

Cora patted Wes's cheek. "'Kay." Then she looked up at April. "I okay, Mommy."

A tear slipped down April's face. She wiped it away. "Good girl."

The tension seeped out of the situation.

Just then Jack Murphy walked toward them. "Joel, who do we have here?" He stopped and nodded toward April. "Ma'am."

"This is Mrs. Landers, her sons, Todd, and Wes. And the little one is Cora."

"So you're the gentlemen who hired Joel away from me for this week." Jack shook the boys' hands. "I'll have to keep my eye on you."

The boys stood up straighter.

Jack turned to April. "I'm glad to meet you. I really liked your father-in-law. Vernon was a good man."

Joel noticed no one mentioned April's husband and wondered why that was.

"Since you're here, I have your check for the

horses and a little something extra." Jack threw Joel a grin.

"I appreciate that."

"If you want to wait at the snack area, I'll be right back. Maybe you can convince Hank to rustle up some chocolate-chip cookies and milk."

"Can we, Mom?" Wes asked.

She hesitated. "Well, I've always had a weakness for chocolate-chip cookies, so lead the way, Mr. Joel."

The boys looked around the rodeo with awe.

"Wow, Mom, this is so cool," Todd whispered as they walked to the concession stand.

Although she gave permission, she fought the irrational fear that her boys might be tempted to follow the rodeo lifestyle when they were grown. And she didn't want to lose any more Landerses to a roaming lifestyle than she had already.

Chapter Five

Joel led the way to the concession area. "Hank, I've got hungry boys and thirsty adults here who need tending," he called out.

A grizzled man of indeterminate age appeared out of the back. He grinned when he saw Joel. "Who do you have with you?"

Joel introduced everyone.

"Howdy, guys. You here for some coffee?" Hank's eyes twinkled.

Wes's face scrunched into a frown. "No, we came to see Helo and Sadie. We wanted to see if they were okay."

"They were at our ranch," Todd added, "and we wanted to be sure they weren't sad to leave us and come to the rodeo."

Hank rubbed his chin. "Good idea. Well, I have fresh chocolate-chip cookies and milk. Will that do?" He turned to April. "Coffee and a cookie?"

"I'd like that."

Hank disappeared into the kitchen while April and the kids settled at one of the picnic tables.

Cora wiggled out of her mother's arms. April set the girl on her feet and she raced around the table to Joel. She stopped by his side and solemnly looked up at him.

"Up." She raised her hands.

With a bag of cookies in one hand and two coffee mugs in the other, Hank stood transfixed, as if he'd never seen a little girl before.

Cora continued holding up her hands.

"Remember, you need to pick her up," Todd informed Joel, breaking into the silence. "She won't quit until she gets her way."

Hank grunted. "Ain't that how it is with females?"

"Cora." April rushed toward her daughter.

Joel scooped up the little girl and tried to set her on the bench. She wasn't interested in leaving his arms.

"It seems you've acquired a girlfriend," Hank said, grinning as he set the mugs and bags of cookies on the table. "And a mighty cute one, too."

April's cheeks reddened. "I'm sorry, I'll take her."

When she tried to scoop up her daughter, the little girl protested.

Joel held up his hand. "It's okay. It isn't every

day such a lovely lady wants me to hold her in my arms."

"You sure? I wouldn't want to embarrass you in front of your friends," April whispered.

"I'm fine with holding Cora." And they weren't just words. He felt a special bond with the little girl, much like his dad would've had when he held his daughter.

Hank grinned. "I'll be back with milk for the kids."

April looked everywhere but at Joel. Cora reached for the cookies. He opened the bag and gave the little munchkin one. The boys also helped themselves to the treats.

"You should try one of these." Joel waved around the cookie. "They're good, but it's his barbecue and potato salad that will stop you in your tracks and make you know you've tasted the best."

"If I didn't know better, Joel Kaye, I'd say you were buttering me up." Hank placed three cartons of milk on the table and filled the mugs with coffee.

"I could use one of those, too," Jack said, pointing to the mug as he walked to the table. He handed April an envelope.

She opened the envelope and looked inside. Slowly, she pulled out the tickets. She threw a puzzled look at Jack and then Joel. "Are these supposed to be in here?"

Jack grinned. "They are. When Joel told me about your boys, well, we wanted them to see the rodeo."

Wes's and Todd's eyes widened.

"Both days?" Wes asked, inching closer to see inside the envelope.

"That's right," Jack confirmed.

Smiles of pure joy lit their faces.

"Yes!" Todd yelled. "We're going to the rodeo."

April stared down at the envelope. Joel watched as several emotions crossed her face—hope, gratefulness and sadness. What was that about?

Whoa, it wasn't his business, he told himself. He was here to gain points with each rodeo toward that championship belt buckle. Only this time around, as he and Hank had commiserated last week, it was a little harder on his body than it was at eighteen. Of course, planting, running that tractor wasn't? Yes, it was, but somehow, someway he felt more energized after a day on the ranch.

The boys happily ate their cookies and asked Jack about the rodeo.

"Are you a cowboy, too, or just a helper?" Todd asked.

April swallowed hard. "I'm sorry, Mr. Murphy. Sometimes children just throw you a surprise."

Two puzzled faces looked at her.

Joel leaned over the table and whispered loudly, "He's the boss."

"Oh." Wes and Todd found their cookies mighty interesting.

Jack's eyes twinkled. "I'm a cowboy who is now the boss. I started competing when I was your age. After high school, I went to college and learned about business. I have my own ranch, wife and family, but when the rodeo owners asked me to manage this circuit of the traveling rodeo, I agreed."

"Can you throw a lariat like Mr. Joel did when he came and got Sadie and Helo?" Todd ventured.

"I can."

"And when is your birthday?"

Jack's brow arched.

"It's important," Joel said.

"October 10."

Todd threw a smirk at his brother. When he turned back, he looked at Joel. "Can you show us how to throw a lariat like you did to get Helo and Sadie?" Todd waited patiently for an answer.

Looking into Wes's and Todd's faces, Joel couldn't ignore their plea. And showing them how to throw would help their dreams.

"Boys, I'd be proud to show you how to throw a lariat. If that's okay with your mom," he tacked on after catching April's frown.

The boys turned to their mother. "Please?"

Their pleading expressions deserved an Academy Award. Joel didn't dare smile, but the little guys were good at making their mother feel guilty.

"You sure?" April asked. "You didn't sign up for tutoring sessions."

"Not a problem." He winked at her. "Okay, boys, let's go learn to throw a lariat."

Cheers went up.

Joel smiled, looking forward to teaching these boys, but April didn't look pleased. Why?

Joel led the little group to the souvenir stand. "Mike, Millie, anyone home?"

An older woman appeared from the back of the stand. "Hey, Joel, what do you have here?" She looked over the counter at the boys.

"I have two budding young cowboys who want to learn to throw a lariat. You got any of those junior lariats?"

Todd and Wes looked up into Millie's eyes, waiting for her answer. April knew her boys could melt the hardest of hearts with their expressions. They'd put "the hurt" on her more than once, and Millie was a pushover.

"I do, but they're in the back. Let me go get them."

The boys bounced like windup toys, waiting for Millie's return.

April stepped forward. "Joel, maybe—"

He smiled at her. "It's okay."

No, it wasn't. She needed to pay for her boys' lariats. It was her responsibility.

Millie appeared with two lariats. "I have just the right thing for these pint-size cowboys." She opened the side door and walked around the front of the booth. "Here you go, gentlemen."

The boys took the ropes as if they were made of gold. Wes grinned. "Thank you."

Joel pulled his wallet out of his back pocket and handed Millie a twenty-dollar bill. She waved him off. "No. It's my treat."

April stepped forward, determined to pay for her boys' lariats. "Thank you, Millie, but I want to pay for these. You need to stay in business yourself." April knew the effect of the lack of money.

The older woman shook her head. "It's my gift. I have grandsons that I don't see often enough."

April opened her mouth, but Wes cut her off. "I have my birthday money, Mom, and chore money at home. I can bring it with me when we come to the rodeo later."

Todd nodded solemnly. "Me, too."

Millie fixed a look on April, her eyebrow raised, questioning if she would object. April's mouth went dry, but she nodded.

"Then you bring me five dollars to pay for the lariats."

"Yes, ma'am," Wes answered.

April fought the emotions threatening to overwhelm her.

Joel cleared his throat. "Now that we've got that business taken care of, let's learn how to throw these and catch us a critter."

Cora reached out her hands. "Horsey." She pointed to the stuffed horse hanging at the back of the booth.

Millie touched the buff-colored stuffed pony and said, "This?"

"Yes."

Taking the horse down, she handed it to the little girl. Cora eagerly accepted the stuffed animal, clutching it to her chest.

"That's my gift," Millie told April before she could object.

"But—"

"Are you going to deny me the joy of sharing my bounty with another?"

The comment cut off April's objection. Was she so determined to provide for her children that she couldn't accept a gift? "No."

Millie cupped Cora's cheek. "You take good care of this horse."

Cora eagerly nodded. "I will."

"Okay, boys, we're going to learn to throw these lariats. Come with me." Joel turned and led them to a concrete spot used as the waiting area for the contestants before they went into the arena. On the way, he grabbed his own lariat.

Several bales of hay stood around the edge of the waiting area. Joel looked for a piece of lumber. Finally, he found the bottom of a sign and jammed it into the hay. April moved to one of the bales, sat and placed Cora beside her.

Joel motioned the boys toward him and questioned them if they knew the names of the different parts of the lariat. The boys knew, explaining their opa had told them the names.

Joel nodded. "My grandfather helped me a lot when I was a little shaver like you. It sounds like your opa was a very wise man."

Both boys beamed with pride.

Over the next half hour, Joel explained how to throw the lariat. Neither boy let his attention drift from the instructions. After Joel lassoed the stick several times, he turned to his eager students.

"Okay, now it's your turn."

Wes went first, and his first attempt had the lasso falling to the ground. His shoulders slumped.

"That was an okay beginning, but you need to relax your wrist and let the lasso start spinning around." Joel demonstrated the technique of using his wrist as an axle, then squatted by Wes and held his wrist. With Joel's hand covering Wes's, they started to swing the lariat overhead. It took several attempts for Wes to get the rope to where he could throw it.

"I think you got it, now try for yourself." Joel stood and backed away.

Wes started to swing the rope and had a good loop.

"Now throw it."

Wes did, but missed. "I can't do this."

Joel squatted down again. "You may have failed this time, but true cowboys don't quit. You practice. Isn't that right, April?"

Joel's question caught her off guard. "Yes. You remember the first time I tried to make Oma's chocolate cake. Was it as good as hers?"

"No," Wes answered. Todd stuck his tongue out.

Joel's eyes twinkled.

"Have I gotten better?"

"Yes," Wes admitted.

"And you asked me to bake that cake on your last birthday, didn't you?"

Wes nodded.

"It's the same way with the lariat."

"Your mom's right. I think it took me three weeks of practice before I roped my first fence post."

"Really?" A note of hope laced Wes's response.

"It takes practice and patience to be a cowboy, but I think you can do it."

Wes thought about Joel's answer. "I can practice."

"Good."

Todd stepped up and tried to throw the lariat, his attempt no better than his brother's.

For the next thirty minutes the boys practiced throwing. By the end of the session, there was a collection of cowboys surrounding them, offering support and help.

Jack walked up, watched the cowboys help the boys, but before long the teaching session came to an end.

April scrambled to her feet. "Boys, it's time to go, but I think you need to thank Mr. Joel and all the cowboys who offered you encouragement."

Both Wes and Todd thanked the men.

Joel walked with them to their truck.

"You've made my sons' week—really, their month."

"It was nothing." He shrugged. "I enjoyed passing along the lessons I learned from my gramps and dad."

April searched his face, wanting to make sure Joel wasn't simply snowing her, but it seemed she'd found a man who meant what he said.

"Thank you." It took several minutes for her to secure all the children in her truck.

"I'll see you tomorrow, early."

"The fields have been planted. If you want to say your obligation is over, I'd understand."

"True, but the boys hired me to help around the ranch for this week, so if you have any major work you need done, make a list. Any fence mending, bridle repair, barn repair. This is the perfect time. Otherwise I'd just be sitting here at the rodeo, bored to death, with nothing to do."

April doubted that, but she could feel her children waiting on her answer, and she had more than enough work to keep him busy. She thought of something and bit her bottom lip to keep from smiling.

"What?"

"I have a couple of bathrooms that could use a good cleaning."

The priceless look on Joel's face made her laugh.

"I'd rather clean out the stables."

"You got it, cowboy."

As they pulled out of the parking space, all three children waved to Joel as if he were their long-lost uncle. Exiting the parking lot, April glanced in her rearview mirror and saw the tall cowboy standing among the few trucks and trailers, watching them.

A longing shot through her. How nice it would be to have someone there all the time whom she could depend on. But if Joel left his ranch to follow the rodeo, he wouldn't be much different from her husband.

The truth dampened her joy.

By eight o'clock that night all three of her children had fallen into bed, dead asleep. She settled on the couch to watch TV, but the show didn't keep her interest and she kept reliving the day.

The boys had talked about Mr. Joel all the way from the arena, through their errands, through dinner.

According to them, Mr. Joel was the "bestest cowboy in the world." Who knew her little boys had that many words and could use them in one afternoon? They were like the ground after a long drought, soaking up the rain of Joel's attention.

She couldn't blame Joel. He was the innocent victim in this scenario. He'd seen a need and worked to fill it. No one had to point out the situation. And Joel seemed to enjoy spending time with the boys, unlike their father, who had found excuses not to be with them.

Her children were crazy about Joel, and he actually got her to have some fun, too. It was all good, but what would happen when the rodeo moved on to the next city? How would the boys survive his loss? Cora? Her?

Joel wasn't trying to worm his way into their lives, but he had.

Benefit versus cost. What to do? She'd already dealt with a man who had a wandering gene. She could pay the cost again, but could her babies? Would it be better for them all to pay the price of losing him, rather than never to have known the joy he brought to their lives?

She didn't have an answer.

* * *

Joel walked by the horse trailer he called home since he had gone back on the circuit. The trailer belonged to his good friend and now brother-in-law, Caleb Jensen. After Caleb's marriage to Joel's sister, Brenda, the couple had encouraged Joel to pursue his dream of getting the championship belt buckle. They'd even insisted Joel use Caleb's horse trailer. For twelve long years it had been Joel's dream to finish out a year on the circuit, working toward that belt buckle.

After he graduated from high school, he'd wanted to follow the circuit for a year to get enough money so he could buy his own ranch, but after his high-school girlfriend and fiancée betrayed him with another man, Joel buried himself in the competition, and soon that drive transformed itself into the goal of winning a championship belt buckle. He'd been one of the top two contenders when his parents were killed in a car accident on New Year's Eve. He drove home the next day. He'd never regretted leaving the rodeo, but now he'd been given a second chance. He didn't intend to squander his opportunity.

Joel stopped by the corral where his horse, Spice, a dapple gray, made her way to the fence, butting his hand, wanting to be petted.

"You miss me?"

Spice lipped the sleeve of his shirt.

"I don't have anything. Sorry."

Spice butted her muzzle against his hand.

"Well, girl, what do you think of spending some time out in a pasture grazing in a field, getting to know a couple of little cowboys and their horses? You'll enjoy yourself. Maybe see how I used to live on my family's ranch. Who knows, you might like it and I'd have a hard time getting you back."

When those boys hired him, it had resonated in his heart. Helping with the ranch work would make him feel useful. And able to give April and her family some relief. He knew he couldn't walk away.

Spice turned and trotted back to the other side of the corral, mingling with the other horses.

"Those are quite some eager cowboys you brought here this afternoon," Jack commented, coming to a stop by Joel.

"You remember when you saw the world with those innocent eyes?"

"Barely." Jack shook his head.

"It's been a while for me, too."

"So, am I going to see you tomorrow, or you going to be out at the Landerses' place?"

"The boys hired me to help plant those fields, but there's work around the place that needs to be done that I doubt April can manage by herself."

"April?"

Joel noted the smirk on Jack's face. "You know what I mean."

"Can't help myself."

Joel ignored the comment. "I'll help at the ranch, since if I stayed here I'd have to look at your ugly mug. Out there, the scenery's better."

Throwing back his head, Jack laughed. "You got me there. If I was in your shoes, I'd want to look at the lady, too."

Joel nodded. "If you need me for any reason, just call."

"I doubt I'll need you with all the other guys hanging around here doing nothing. I think you'll be needed more out at the Landerses' place."

"Thanks."

"No problem."

Walking back to his trailer, Joel found himself eager to be back out at the ranch, which surprised him. Now the question he faced was, why was he so eager? Was it the ranch and the familiar work or the special lady and her children that he wanted to see?

Chapter Six

Joel arrived at the Landerses' ranch a little after seven. By the time he had his mare unloaded, the kitchen door had slammed several times and all three children stood on the porch, watching.

Todd wrapped his arms over the railing and stepped on the bottom crossbar to see better. "Why'd you bring a horse? You want to give us that horse?"

"No. I brought my horse, Spice, to give her some time to graze out in the field with Buckwheat and Sammie. She doesn't get the chance just to walk around and eat grass and be fat and happy."

Cora clutched her stuffed horse. "My horsey." She pointed toward Spice. "You horsey?"

"You're right, Miss Cora. This is my horse, and she's going to visit you." Joel led Spice toward the paddock where Sammie and Buckwheat grazed.

April stepped out of the house. "Breakfast should be ready in twenty minutes, which should give you and the boys time to feed the stock."

"Aw, Mom," Todd complained.

"Do you want to eat?" Joel asked.

"Yeah," Wes answered.

"So do your horses and the rest of the animals, so don't you think we should feed them, too?"

Todd folded his arms over his chest. "Why can't the animals wait?"

"Well, does Sammie have hands to open the grain bags or the barrel where the feed is kept?"

"Of course not." Todd giggled.

"But you do."

The boys nodded.

"Then we can open bags, scoop out oats and care for the animals the good Lord has given us. And if I remember my Sunday school lessons right, the Lord put us in charge of the animals, so it's your job to care for them, just like it's your mom's job to care for you boys till you get grown."

Both Wes and Todd thought about what Joel said.

"Make sense?" Joel asked.

Todd nodded. "I remember something Opa said when it was snowing hard and bad outside. He said the good Lord gave him a job and it's our responsibility to do it. I guess that's what he was talking about."

"Your opa was a wise man. So let's finish our chores so the workers can eat, too."

As April put the last of the sausage patties on the table, the boys walked inside.

"Oh, that smells great," Joel said, stopping, closing his eyes and inhaling deeply. When he surveyed the table, he smiled. "Blueberry pancakes?"

"With homemade blueberry syrup and fresh-churned butter," April added. She felt silly touting the goodies set out for them to eat, but the words tumbled out of her mouth before she thought.

"Is that Mrs. Johnson's butter?" Todd asked, looking at the crock, then back at his mother.

April flushed. "It is."

"Is this a special occasion?"

"I thought Mr. Joel might like to taste some of Mrs. Johnson's butter."

"Yes." Todd made a fist and brought his elbow down and to his side.

The boys started to sit when Joel shook his head. "Hand washing."

The two tromped to the bathroom behind Joel without a single complaint and returned in record time.

"Then let's sit down and eat while it's warm."

Wes started for the pancakes when April said, "Wes, you want to pray for our food?"

"Lord, thank You for the good food Mama cooked and the extra special stuff she set for breakfast this morning. And thanks for Mr. Joel to help us. Amen."

"Amen," April whispered. Lifting her head, she saw the strong, handsome cowboy who took her breath away sitting across the table. She wanted to pinch herself to make sure she wasn't dreaming, because no one like Joel, a man in his mid-thirties whom her children adored and who spent the time to teach them, had ever sat there before. Their father never had. Sure, their grandparents tried, but it didn't make up for their father ignoring them.

Not only did Joel connect with her kids, but he made her dream crazy dreams like the happily-ever-after kind of dream.

"Mom, I need some butter," Wes announced, breaking into her silly thoughts.

April held up the crock. "And we say—"

"Please."

She spent the next several minutes helping Cora fix her pancakes. When April checked to see if Todd had managed to fix his, she saw Joel helping her son. The man kept her off guard with his thoughtful little gestures. If he'd tried to flatter her or act like the big famous cowboy star, she could've ignored him. But he didn't. Instead he did small, considerate things that slipped under the barrier she'd built around her heart.

Joel took the first bite of his pancake and paused. "Oh, that's good. I haven't had something that good since my grandma made her blueberry coffee cake for our Easter breakfast."

"Mom, can I have more syrup?" Wes asked.

She handed him the bottle.

"What are you going to do today, Mr. Joel?" Wes asked as he poured the syrup.

"I saw some things in the barn that need tending. If you have anything you can think needs to be done around the house, April, I can do that—except those bathrooms we talked about. I'd just be sitting around doing nothing back at the rodeo. And I want the boys to get their money's worth."

Her first inclination was to tell him to go back to the rodeo, they didn't need him, but she knew that wasn't true. Those silly dreams she'd been spinning worried her, but she needed all the help she could get—and she could ignore her fantasies.

"How long have you been a cowboy?" Todd asked.

Cora's piece of pancake fell off her fork and she solved the problem by picking it up and stuffing it into her mouth.

"Cora."

April's and Joel's hands collided over Cora's plate. April sat back down, allowing him to wipe the little girl's hand clean.

"Let's see, you asked me how long I've been a cowboy."

Wes nodded.

"A long time."

"How long is that?"

"On my last birthday, which you know was the beginning of this month, I turned thirty-four."

The boys, wide-eyed and mouths agape, looked at each other.

"Why, that's almost as old as Mr. Moore," Todd sputtered.

April's fork stopped midway to her mouth. She fought a laugh.

Joel cleared his throat. "I think Mr. Moore is a little older than me. Of course, there are days…"

April read the rest of his thought—that he sometimes felt as old as Mr. Moore.

"You been with the rodeo *that* long?" Todd asked.

Joel laughed. "I didn't join the rodeo when I was three."

Snickers sounded around the table.

"This time I've been traveling with them a little over a year."

"Done," Cora announced.

April immediately stood and wiped Cora's hands and face before taking her out of the booster seat.

"Well, I think it's time to stop talking and start working," Joel said.

After plates were put in the sink, the boys headed to the bathroom.

"April, if you'll make a list of what else needs to be done, I'll start on it and see how much I can get to over the next couple of days."

She studied him, trying to decipher his motives. "Okay."

"I'll start in the barn, then check back with you in a bit." He walked out of the house, leaving April gawking.

"Where's Mr. Joel?" Wes asked.

"In the barn."

Both boys raced out of the kitchen.

April's legs gave way. Who was this man? And why was he here?

You prayed. The thought popped into her head.

Yes, but—but what?

Joel had lived up to his word. His attitude confused her and challenged her assumptions about him. Wasn't he a man who traveled with the rodeo and didn't stay in one place long enough to let the dust settle around him? Didn't he have a wandering gene, just like Ross?

But his attitude didn't resemble her husband's in any way. Nothing about Joel made sense.

Who was this man? She had no satisfactory answers.

The day passed quickly. After breakfast, April sat down and made a list of the things that hadn't been done in a couple of years, due to Grace's breast cancer and Vernon's heart attack.

The boys stuck to Joel like glue, never letting the man out of their sight. Laughter drifted out of the barn, and as soon as Cora woke up from her morning nap, she wanted to join the boys, which meant April had to go out to the barn.

"Hey, Miss Cora, what are you doing out here?" Joel asked.

April followed with water and plastic cups. "Anyone thirsty?"

The boys hurried to her side.

She held up the jug. "Want any?"

Joel stared at the kid-size cups and his eyebrow arched.

April fought her giggles. "Sorry."

"As long as you don't tell the other guys on the circuit I drank water out of this—" he held up the kiddie cup "—I'm good."

"I can do that." She poured him a cup of water.

His hand wrapped around the kiddie cup, dwarfing it. He frowned but drank the water.

"Mom, that's too small for Mr. Joel," Wes explained.

"I'll remember next time."

Wes shook his head. "Girls."

"Do you have a list for me, April?" Joel asked.

Hearing him say her name made her stomach jump.

She handed him the list.

After reading it, he added another couple of chores, with which she agreed.

The balance of the day, they all worked as a team with a pause for lunch.

It was the best afternoon April had had since— well, she couldn't think of another afternoon.

How pathetic was that?

The day passed quickly and after dinner, the boys begged for Joel to join them in a game before he left. It had been a long time since he'd played a board game, but with April's encouragement, he agreed.

The kids laughed when Joel tried to sit on the floor.

"These boots weren't made for sitting cross-legged."

"I can," Todd announced, plopping down in front of the coffee table.

"Well, I'm not as young as you, so my bones won't move as easily as yours," Joel teased.

April solved the problem when she pushed the leather ottoman close to the table, which Joel sat on to play the game.

After several minutes of play, Joel spun the spinner to see how many blocks he should move. The next move fell to April, but she only got a two, much to her sons' delight. She shrugged off the bad move. Joel admired her teasing attitude. Here was a woman who wasn't afraid to get her hands dirty, as she'd demonstrated earlier by pitching in with the hard work in the barn. His mom and grandma were like that. Lately, he'd run into too many ladies who enjoyed playing cowgirl, but if it affected their nail polish, well, forget it.

"Dinner was mighty good, April. When you cook for yourself, you appreciate when someone else does the cooking."

"So, did you cook for yourself?" Wes asked as he took his turn.

"When Gramps and I had to do the cooking ourselves, we used a Crock-Pot, but it's nice to have someone else in charge. And your mom does a good job."

Both boys grinned at their mother.

"When my sister came back to the ranch, well, she refused to be the only one responsible for dinner. She'd been in the army for over ten years."

The boys' eyes widened.

"We each had days when it was our turn to cook. 'Course, if you didn't cook, you cleaned up. No one got away without pitching in. So when you help your mom with the dishes, remember that a captain in the army did the same."

It took less than five minutes to conclude the game.

"We need to check on the horses and finish

any chores that need to be done before I leave for the night."

The boys grew somber as they put away the game.

"Thank you," April whispered as he set the game box on the coffee table.

"No problem. Seeing dinner through the eyes of the person preparing it gives you a different perspective."

"I like that. Your sister sounds like a great gal."

"She is."

"And you'll make some lady a great husband, thanks to your sister." April stood there for a moment, her eyes wide, her Freudian slip echoing through her mind. "Uh, what I meant was—"

He chuckled. "Like I said, I've been the cook. Any help is welcomed."

"That it is."

"C'mon, boys. Let's go feed the animals and check on things out in the barn before I load Spice in her trailer and drive back to the rodeo."

The words burst the pleasant mood, reminding everyone that he had other obligations at the rodeo that he needed to do.

The boys proved to be a help with the chores, with less direction required each time. They were learning the daily routine of the ranch and understanding what each animal required. After finishing, they went inside to get ready for bed. Joel called to Spice, wanting to load her into her horse trailer. Her ears perked up, she looked over her shoulder, then went back to grazing.

"It appears she's not listening to you."

Joel turned in the direction of April's voice. She walked to where he stood beside the pasture fence.

"I think the charm of your pasture outweighs anything I could say. I bought Spice from a friend who was retiring from rodeo when I started back out on the circuit. Spice was used to the traveling and working the rodeo shows, as opposed to my horse I used on the ranch. She knew the ropes. Now, suddenly, she wants to just hang out in the pasture."

"I guess even horses want a few days off."

"I could leave the trailer here, but my bed is in the front compartment."

"It seems you've got a dilemma."

Todd appeared on the porch. "Mr. Joel, could you stop by my room before you leave and say good-night?"

April pressed her lips together.

"Do you have an objection to that?" He didn't want to upset her family rituals.

"Yes."

He opened his mouth to respond when she answered, "He'll be there in a couple of minutes, Todd."

The lady sent mixed signals, confusing him.

"What just happened here?"

She folded her hands over her chest. "I know when I can't stop a sandstorm."

He frowned. "What?"

"Living out here, when you see a sandstorm on the horizon, there's nothing you can do but take cover. I feel like I'm watching as a storm comes my way and I can only ride out the aftereffects. When you leave, there won't be a man to tuck my boys into bed at night. They'll have to settle for their mom." She sighed. "Vernon always kissed the kids good-night."

She didn't paint a good picture.

"What about their dad?"

Her lips tightened, but she didn't answer.

"I'm sorry. It's not my business."

"Their father was never interested in coming home after he left to work on different oil rigs. He begged my dad to get him a position on an oil platform out in the Gulf. It was more exciting than staying on the ranch with his family and working."

Joel didn't know how to walk this situation back. His first girlfriend had claimed he never thought about her feelings. Here in this situation, he didn't have a clue. He'd rather face a mad bull. He knew how to respond to that. "Is it okay to say good-night to the boys?"

A short laugh drifted into the night. "Sorry for the confusion. Say good-night. It's a treat for them, which I can't deny."

He felt her confusion. "You sure?"

"I don't want to deny them this special time."

Although she was worried, she put her boys first, which won Joel's admiration. Someday, he'd like a family like this. Maybe have boys like Wes and Todd. And several girls like Cora. "Okay, I'll say good-night to them as soon as I load up my horse."

"Hope you get her into the trailer. Spice doesn't seem interested in leaving." Winking, she walked back into the house.

April sat in her office, catching up with her mail and messages. She heard Joel walk down the hall and enter the boys' room. She couldn't hear the exact exchange between them, but she heard the boys' laughter.

The sound made her want to smile and cry at the same time. Why couldn't her boys experience that joy every night? She'd done everything right, but—

She clamped down on the pity party.

"I'll be back tomorrow." Joel stood in the doorway of her office. "So continue to think of chores you need done."

"You sure you're going to be here tomorrow?" Wes called out.

Joel turned and walked back to the boys' room.

April hurried after him, concerned at Joel's reaction.

He stopped at the boys' door. "I gave my word, Wes. I'll be here."

There wasn't a hint of annoyance or impatience in his voice or attitude.

"Okay."

Joel moved toward her.

Relief and gratitude washed over her. Moisture gathered in April's eyes. "You'll have to excuse the boys. When their father was home, they couldn't count on him to tuck them into bed. Vernon took over the job. How my in-laws managed to raise such a st—" She clamped her mouth shut.

"Good night." He turned and walked down the hall.

She took a deep breath, dumbfounded she'd said so much to Joel. He didn't need to know about the ugly part of her life. About the selfish and unreliable husband she'd married. She couldn't blame his parents after knowing them. She was the one who'd married Ross. His callous actions had hurt his parents as much as they'd hurt her.

She stepped into her office but heard movement in the hall. She turned but didn't see anything. She waited, her curiosity driving her. Finally, Joel sneaked out of Cora's room.

"She was asleep and I wasn't going to wake her."

The man kept confusing her with his concern for her children. Why would a man who had only been with them less than a week concern himself with kissing her daughter good-night?

"Thank you."

"I'll leave as soon as I coax my horse into her trailer."

"Use some of that charm you cowboys are so famous for on that female."

"Whoever told you that doesn't know what they are talking about."

Her eyes widened at his abrupt response. He strode past her, saying nothing. She heard him cross the living room and move through the kitchen. The back door didn't slam but closed firmly. Whatever had she said that irritated him? Sometimes men took offense so much easier than women. Go figure.

"'Use some of that charm you cowboys are so famous for,'" he grumbled to himself. "What does she know about cowboy charm?" He strode out to the pasture where Spice grazed. Stopping at the fence, he called to her again.

The horse ignored him.

He stared out at Spice. Never, in all the time Joel had owned her, had he had a problem. She didn't fail him in the calf roping—always shot eagerly out of the gate after the calf. So why had his horse suddenly grown contrary?

He walked to the horse trailer and opened the side door to his bunk and pulled open the door to the compartment where he kept some peppermint. Back at the fence, he unwrapped the peppermint and called out. Buckwheat trotted up to Joel. He closed his hand. "That's not for you, boy." Buckwheat nudged his fist. After a moment, Joel opened his hand and gave the peppermint to Buckwheat.

"You lost your treat," Joel called out to his horse. Spice wasn't going to leave. He could run after her, but maybe the best way to deal with this out-of-control girl was to leave her for the night. Maybe after a day or two she'd be willing to start working again.

He turned his back and rested against the fence. Reaching into his shirt pocket, he fished out his cell and called Jack.

"I'm running a little late out here, Jack. I'll be there in about fifteen minutes to help with the evening chores."

"That's okay, Joel. Why don't you stay out there and not worry about it? I've got enough help here to take care of everything. Forget about driving back and forth each day. I'll just expect you Sunday evening."

Jack's suggestion solved his problem. "I signed on to help and—"

"Have you heard of a favor, Kaye? Since you're helping the lady rancher, I can contribute, too, and not have her ranch hand running back and forth daily."

"You mean I shouldn't look a gift horse in the mouth?"

"You're catchin' on, cowboy."

That cowboy thing again. "Thanks, Jack. I'll mention it to the lady."

"Good. See you Sunday."

Joel disconnected the call and turned toward the pasture. "Well, Spice, you might have gotten your way. I guess I need to check with April on the change of plans."

He walked back into the kitchen.

She stood in front of the refrigerator, a carton of buttermilk in her hand. She held it up. "Want some?"

"To drink?"

"Yes. It's good to settle one's stomach."

His grandmother used to drink it on a regular basis, but he couldn't understand that. "Uh, no. Thanks." Closing the refrigerator door, she leaned back against it. "Is something wrong? You're not coming back tomorrow?"

She didn't have much confidence in a man's

word. "No, I'll be here. Actually, if you don't mind, I'll spend the night in my compartment in the horse trailer. It seems Spice doesn't want to leave."

April stood there staring at him for a moment, then a snort caused her to choke on her buttermilk. Placing the glass on the counter, she coughed. He patted her on the back. Wiping her tears, she tried to catch her breath. Joel stepped back, not knowing what to do.

"So your horse is running the show?"

He shrugged. "That's it. The female isn't cooperating." He felt dumber than the tree stump they used for chopping wood at his parents' ranch. "I'm thinking Spice is enjoying herself too much." He shrugged. "I could catch her, but it's not often she gets the opportunity to graze in a field. Do you mind if I just sleep in my trailer? I didn't want to surprise you."

"No, I don't mind." She finished her buttermilk, washed out the glass and put it in the sink. "See you tomorrow."

"Good night."

"He couldn't catch his horse." Joel heard the words drift back to him as she walked down the hall.

Once back in his trailer he pulled off his boots and stretched out on his bunk. He could've caught Spice, if he was honest with himself. Maybe his horse knew he wasn't serious about her coming to him and them leaving. Maybe she wanted to stay here to soak up the ranch life.

He didn't blame her.

Chapter Seven

The smell of coffee drew April down the hall to the kitchen. April's mother-in-law had said the best invention since the automatic washing machine was a timed coffeemaker. April had to agree.

Grace had lived up to her name. She'd taken April under her wing and taught her about ranching and the demands on a ranch wife, which meant she helped wherever she was needed, but her main responsibility was to have food ready for folks when they came in from the range or chasing down cows.

Padding into the kitchen, April headed straight for the mugs above the coffeemaker. On her way there, she caught sight of the horse trailer parked by the barn. She pulled out two mugs. Joel would probably want a shot of caffeine, too, to start his day.

As she poured coffee, April found herself

smiling. Joel had surprised her last night when he'd asked if she minded if he just spent the night in his trailer, since he couldn't pry his horse away from the pasture.

His thoughtfulness and change of plans unsettled her. In spite of her tiredness, she'd lain awake, sleep the last thing on her mind. The boys would be delighted to find Joel here. Cora, too. Having him at the ranch made her heart want things that couldn't be. What would it be like to have help all the time, not only when she called for it or the church knew her need?

And wasn't he handsome?

Her mind shied away from answering that question. It wasn't worth dwelling on. Joel Kaye was only here for a couple of days, and she needed to remember that.

She heard the sound of boots walking across the porch, then the screen door opened, snapping her back to the here and now.

"I thought I smelled coffee."

She held up a mug and turned. In three steps, he was by her side and took the mug. After his first swallow, he paused, enjoying the taste.

"This is the right way to begin the day."

As she looked into his eyes, suddenly Joel's words took on a different meaning.

"That's good."

She swallowed. "Most of the ranch hands I know can't start their working day without a cup of joe. I'll start on breakfast and it should be ready by the time morning chores are done."

Small footsteps pounded down the hall. Wes, Todd and Cora, clutching her new horse, stood in the doorway. All were in their jammies.

"Wow, you got here early," Wes commented.

"I spent the night in my trailer."

Wes's eyes widened. "Really?"

"Yup, and I'm ready to work."

Wes took a step toward him.

"I could use help, but you have to be dressed in your boots."

Two little bodies zipped down the hall. Cora moved toward her mother's leg.

Swallowing the last of his coffee, Joel placed it on the counter. He squatted down to Cora's level. "You going to help me, too?"

Cora buried her face in her mother's leg.

"Give her until after she eats. Of all my three children, Cora is my slow starter."

Joel reached out and mussed Cora's hair. "I'll see you at breakfast." He stood. "And you be sure to take care of that horse of yours."

The screen slammed behind him, leaving April a moment to gather her scattered thoughts. Within a minute, Wes and Todd ran through the kitchen, stuffing their shirts into their jeans. They didn't say anything, but followed Joel out to the barn.

Scooping up her daughter, April walked down

the hall toward her bedroom. "Let's get you dressed and start breakfast. We're going to have to feed hungry cowboys when they show up in the kitchen."

The thought made her smile.

April was putting a dump cake in the oven later that afternoon when she heard a truck pull up and stop. She moved to the window to see who was here.

Kelly Baker, her good friend and fellow church member, saw her and waved. She hurried up the steps and opened the kitchen screen door.

"I was driving by and thought I'd stop and talk about Sunday's lunch on the ground after service." Kelly shrugged. "And my hunger got the better of me, and I thought I'd see if you have any cookies or crackers for a pregnant lady to eat."

The news caught April by surprise. "Really?"

Kelly beamed. "Yes." April hugged her friend. "I just visited my doctor. I was fortunate they worked me in. When I told him my symptoms, he asked if I could be pregnant. I felt so dumb. I have three babies already." She shook her head. "I haven't even told Dave yet. I wanted to tell my best friend first."

"Your husband might disagree with you."

"Naw. Dave will be excited no matter when I tell him."

"I'm so glad for you. I couldn't be happier."

"You sure?" Kelly's gaze searched April's.

"I am. You were there for me at Cora's birth." Due to complications April could no longer have kids, but she rejoiced with Kelly having another child.

April grabbed a cookie and poured her friend a glass of milk.

Looking at the glass of milk, Kelly frowned.

"If you're pregnant, you need milk more than coffee."

"So you're going to mother me?"

"Yup. I'm going to help your mom keep you on the right track."

Kelly noticed the oven on. "What are you cooking for tomorrow?"

"Dump cake. Along with ham, I'm also bringing hot dogs and potato salad so I know that my boys will have something to eat."

Kelly listened to the quiet. "Where are your boys?"

"They're out with the cowboy they hired to help plant my fields after Al got hurt."

Kelly's mouth flopped open like a fish's. If April wasn't so aware of Joel, she would've thought Kelly's reaction funny. "Why didn't I know about this?" Kelly stood and walked to the back door. "So does that horse trailer belong to your new ranch hand?"

"Yes."

Kelly grinned. "What's this ranch hand look like?"

April shrugged but felt her face betray her with color.

A grin split Kelly's face. "Fess up."

"He looks like a regular cowboy," April answered.

"Is he tall, short, young, old? Give me some details," Kelly demanded.

"He looks like a regular cowboy with dark hair and a nice smile."

The longer Kelly studied her friend's face the bigger her grin became. "Oh, he's a looker, is that what you're telling me?"

"I don't know where you got that idea," April sputtered.

"From that blush on your face. Is he going to come with you to church Sunday?"

"I hadn't planned on it."

Kelly leaned over the table. "Ask him. All cowboys need to be in church and hear the preacher."

"I'll invite him, but why don't we talk about the lunch and make sure we have everything covered?" April didn't want to talk about Joel anymore. She felt exposed by her friend's observations and didn't want to deal with the issues Kelly brought up.

Joel drove up to the barn from the field where they'd just finished fixing an uprooted fence post. The boys told him about the bad storm they had a couple of weeks ago. When he was plowing the fields, he noticed some suspicious-looking fence posts along the edges of the fields. They fixed one this morning.

Both Wes and Todd rode in the cab with him. He noticed the truck parked by the back door.

"I wonder what Mrs. Baker is doing here," Wes said.

"Who is Mrs. Baker?"

"That's Mom's friend," Todd answered. "We go to church with her family. Sunday we're going to bring lunch to church and all eat together."

"Do you go to church?" Wes asked.

"I do. Sometimes the preacher makes it to the rodeo and holds service on Sunday morning."

Wes's brow wrinkled. "Will he have service Sunday?"

"No."

"Then you should come with us and have lunch with the people at the church."

Todd turned and looked up at him, waiting for an answer.

Joel felt like an intruder and didn't think April would like him going with the family. "I'm not sure your mom would want me to go with you."

Todd's eyes widened. "Of course she wants you to come. She's always telling us to invite people and be a 'flection of Jesus."

"A 'flection?" Joel puzzled over the word.

"A reflection of Jesus," Wes clarified.

Stated that way, there was no way he could say no.

"Then I'd be pleased to go to church with you."

A cheer went up. After parking the truck, he helped both boys out of the cab.

"Mom, Mom," Wes called out as he clambered up the stairs.

April, with Cora in her arms, and another woman appeared at the kitchen door. "You finished with your chores?"

Wes and Todd stopped. "Yes, and we invited Mr. Joel to church on Sunday. And he accepted. He's going to eat lunch with us and meet people at the church."

April looked at Joel.

"Isn't that good, Mama?" Todd's chest puffed out. "We did just what you told us to do—bring people to church."

"Aren't you proud of us?" Wes asked.

The woman next to April smiled. "I know your mom is proud of you two." She turned to Joel and reached out her hand. "I'm Kelly Baker, April's best friend. And fellow church member. And you are?"

"This is Mr. Joel Kaye," Wes said. "Todd and I hired him to help around here while the rodeo animals take a spring vacation."

With each word, Kelly's smile broadened. "I think you did a wonderful job, boys." She turned to April and some message passed between them. "I'll see you Sunday, April, and you, too, Mr. Kaye." Kelly hurried to her car. "Thanks for the snack. You're a lifesaver. Now I'll make it home."

The boys waved at Kelly as she drove away, then clambered into the kitchen.

Joel walked up the steps and came face-to-face with April. "I hope you don't mind the boys inviting me to church."

"No, why would I be upset? I'm proud of them. It's good to know their hearts are in the right place. I know you'll enjoy the service."

"Mom," Wes yelled.

"I'm coming."

Joel stood rooted to the ground. After a few steps, she paused, looking over her shoulder. "C'mon. I have fresh coffee and cookies. And if I know cowboys, you're hungry."

He was. And cookies sounded mighty good.

With the boys and Cora finally settled in bed, April walked out of the house, a restlessness running through her. A cool breeze washed over the land, bringing the scent of the fresh-turned earth.

She heard a noise and saw Joel leaning on the fence, looking out into the night. Good. She needed to talk to him without little ears around.

When she was halfway to the fence, he turned and watched her.

"It's a nice night." He closed his eyes and tipped his head back.

"I've always loved spring. Here on the ranch, it becomes such a time of renewal. Lots of babies being born." Kelly came to mind and her joy at having another baby. A sadness touched April's soul. Because of complications during Cora's birth, she'd never have another baby, and her heart ached.

"There's nothing better than seeing a new foal in the stall with the mare," he added.

"You're right." The first time she'd seen a mare give birth, April couldn't stop talking about it. Ross had brought her home to have dinner, and one of the mares went into labor. Thankfully, it had been a Friday night, and she'd sat in the stall, witnessing the birth. Vernon had stayed with her when Ross disappeared. The next morning, she'd asked him where he'd gone. He'd told her he'd seen a birthing before and wasn't interested. Ross's answer should've warned her, but April had ignored it.

Now she stood beside Joel, looking out at the field.

"There's nothing better than seeing an hours-old foal in the stall with its dam."

Her heart swelled hearing him voice the feelings that so agreed with hers. After several moments of silence, April smiled. "I hope you don't feel trapped into going to church with us."

A chuckle escaped his mouth. "I don't. If the traveling preacher would've been here tomorrow, I'd have invited the boys to the cowboy church service Charlie Newman holds. I know your kids would love it. I think you might enjoy it, too. Charlie plans to be this way next week. Maybe your family might like to experience the cowboy service."

"I'd like that."

"Good, we could plan that. But I'm okay going with you tomorrow." He leaned back against the fence. "Todd did surprise me, but you've got two boys there that you should be proud of."

"That's one thing I can say—parenting is never dull. Just when you think you get a handle on it, bam, it all changes." Since she didn't have any siblings, she wished Ross or his cousin Chad were here for her to talk to about how to deal with the boys' needs, but then, Ross probably wouldn't have wanted to talk at all about the boys. Her mother-in-law had helped before she got sick, but afterward, April couldn't bring herself to burden Grace with her questions. And when cousin Chad moved to Montana after Ross's death to get married, she missed talking to him.

"Life's that way. You think you've got it covered, then something happens and turns it all around."

Those were words of experience April heard

coming out of Joel's mouth. She wanted to ask him about it but remembered he would be gone in a couple of days. She didn't want to get any more involved with a man who wasn't going to stick around.

"Tomorrow I'll ride out and finish checking your fields and cattle. The boys told me about the storm a couple of weeks ago, and I noticed more fence posts that need to be checked. I should've done that earlier, but your boys kept me busy."

"Sounds good." She wanted to stand out here longer and talk, review the day, the overall plans for the ranch, but she knew it wasn't appropriate to share such intimate details of her life with him. "I'll make sure to fix you a lunch you can take with you."

His smile nearly brought her to her knees. "Thanks."

She nodded and headed inside before she said something stupid.

The boys were disappointed they couldn't ride out with Joel the next morning.

"Maybe you could practice throwing your lariats," Joel suggested.

Before any complaining could be registered, the telephone rang.

"Help," Kelly said when April answered. "My kids are driving me crazy. Can you bring yours over so they can play?"

April turned to the boys. "Do you want to go to the Bakers' and play this morning?"

"Tell them Greg has the newest game with drag racers. Thunder Alley."

April relayed the message. They nodded. "I'll drive them to your house if you'll drive them back."

"Thank you." Kelly hung up.

"Let me make Joel's lunch and then we'll go over to the Bakers'."

Everyone exited the kitchen, leaving April to pack a lunch for Joel. It felt much too personal, but she shook off the silliness. She'd packed lunches before. It was simply making a ham sandwich with all the vegetables. When she finished, she walked outside and handed Joel the brown bag and thermos.

"Hope you packed coffee."

His teasing broke down the wall she'd been building. "You wouldn't choke if it was just water."

"No, but I'd have to turn in my true-blue cowboy card."

"Don't let Todd hear you say that."

They shared a smile.

"Do you have saddlebags?" April asked. "Vernon's are just inside the barn doors if you need some."

Joel shook his head and grinned. "I don't use those too much when competing."

The screen slammed. "Whatcha doing out there, Mom?" Todd asked.

"Giving Mr. Joel his lunch."

"We're ready, except Cora. She put her shoes on the wrong feet," Todd explained.

April turned. "Why didn't you help?"

Todd's eyes went wide and his mouth fell open. "You want me to do that?"

"I've got to go."

Joel and April traded smiles and went different directions.

All the other fence posts around the Landerses' ranch turned out okay. He could tell that place had been well cared for by April's father-in-law. He also found cattle near a stock pond on the property, and all of the animals looked to be in good shape.

Joel stopped by one of the stock ponds and allowed Spice to drink, then rode her to a spot under a cluster of trees. He dismounted and ground tied Spice, allowing her to graze.

"Now, I'm going to trust you, girl. You're good in the arena, but we haven't tried out in the field. If you decide to bolt, I'll be walking back to the barn."

Spice nodded her head.

"I'll take that as a yes." He pulled the lunch bag and thermos from the saddlebags and settled under a tree.

He didn't want to admit to himself that working this week brought back a lot of good memories of growing up. He saw in April's boys part of himself. He'd never been patient and had always wanted to learn more. He missed his family and needed to call home soon. Maybe what he needed was a family of his own.

The thought startled him.

The work this week had been satisfying, from plowing the fields to riding these fences, making him nostalgic. His dad would've laughed himself silly to know how Joel had enjoyed the work after all the complaining he did as a teen. Who would've thought? But there it was. He enjoyed the ranch work. But the most satisfying part of the week had been sharing meals with April and her children. This situation, he reminded himself, was only temporary. Nothing more. But later, he could see himself with a family very similar to this one. He could just envision a child that would look like April, but with his eyes and her determination.

He shook his head. Wow, was the sun getting to him? That had to be it.

Later that night, after April put the kids to bed, she found Joel outside, sitting on her porch swing. The air still held a nip in it. She shivered. "Are you still okay with coming to church?" She sat next to him on the swing.

"I am."

She shivered again and thought about going inside for a sweater—or she could scoot closer to Joel's warmth. She stiffened her spine. She'd only be out here for a couple of minutes. "Sunday school is at nine-thirty, but I'll see you at breakfast tomorrow morning."

"I don't have any sort of suit. Is that okay?"

"You got a nice shirt and jeans?"

He nodded.

"That will do. But clean boots are a must." She felt stupid warning him, but she'd seen more than one man being noticed for dirt and other stuff on his boots.

"My mom would've grabbed me by the scruff of my neck if I had dirty boots when we went to church. And Grandma would've found her yardstick and educated me."

A cold breeze kicked up, making her grit her teeth. She glanced at him.

"What?"

"Aren't you a little cold?" She shivered.

"No." He patted the place next to him. "Scoot over. I promise to behave myself."

She didn't question it, but slid across the slats to sit beside him. He didn't try to put his arm around her, but left it resting on the back of the swing.

His warmth and closeness drove away the cold and most of her thoughts. "The boys will introduce you around, so no one will criticize your dress. You'll probably get handshakes and back slaps and lots of questions."

"Then I'm up for it."

She wanted to talk to him about more, about other things, but she needed to back off. He'd only be here another day or so. "As long as you're okay with church, that's what I wanted to know."

He went still, as if waiting for her to say something more.

"Good night."

Later, as she snuggled into her bed, April found herself thinking about Joel and going to church with him and her kids. Just like a real family.

Chapter Eight

The moment April parked her truck in the church parking lot, the boys scrambled out of the backseat. "Be careful. Lots of people are arriving." In the next ten minutes, the parking lot would be two-thirds full.

"Out, Mommy," Cora demanded.

Joel felt funny about having April drive, but she had the car seats in her truck and it only made sense for them to use her vehicle.

After April released Cora from her car seat, the little girl made a beeline for him and he scooped her up.

Putting down the tailgate, April picked up the padded carry tote that held her cake and rolls inside. She also had a second tote with ham, hot dogs and potato salad. Joel took the strap and slipped it over his free shoulder.

"Lead the way."

After a moment's hesitation, she nodded and

walked into the church. The boys sauntered beside them, waving and smiling at everyone as if they were stars in a parade.

Once inside the church, a boy the same height and age as Wes pulled him aside. "Who is that?" His whisper qualified as a shout as he pointed at Joel.

"He's with the rodeo, but Todd and me hired him to help at the ranch."

The boy's jaw dropped. It was just the beginning of many questions.

When April dropped the boys off at their Sunday school classes, they let her know they wanted to go to the big people's service today instead of children's church.

Walking away from the first-graders' room, April turned to Joel. "I've volunteered to help with Cora's class for the first service, but I'll walk you down to my class and introduce you."

He stopped. "I'll be happy to help here."

April wasn't sure she heard correctly. "In the two-year-old class?"

"Yes."

"Uh, I don't know if Martha will let you help since they don't know you."

Martha overheard their exchange. "I'm several helpers down, so if Joel would stand at the window and check in the children, that would help." She explained the check-in system.

"Sounds great."

Joel didn't miss a beat and managed to greet each parent who dropped off a child. By the time they made it to the second service, Joel had been introduced to almost everyone in the church. The pastor's wife came by where April, Joel and the children sat waiting for the service to begin and introduced herself.

"You plan to stay for our lunch on the ground?" Leslie Martin asked.

"He's going to be here. Wes and I invited him," Todd explained.

"Good. I'd love to talk with you, and I know my husband will, too, at the lunch."

April panicked. She didn't need the pastor and his wife vetting Joel as if he was a potential suitor. She opened her mouth to protest when someone called out to Leslie.

"Coming." She smiled at Joel, but something in Leslie's smile warned they were watching him. "Nice meeting you, and I look forward to our chat." She hurried off.

April studied her hands.

"It's okay. I'm not offended."

Her head jerked up. She wanted to argue with his assumption, but the twinkle in his eye let her know he knew the truth. "They just want me to find someone. They knew the family. This congregation has been there for the kids and me with each death."

"Good."

She blushed.

"It's good to know that your church has been there for you. That's what church is all about."

She wanted to ask how he knew, but the singers stepped onto the platform and started a praise chorus. Everyone stood and began to sing. Joel didn't look at the words on the screen at the front of the auditorium but knew the chorus and encouraged the children to sing, too. Her view of him as just a cowboy blowing with the wind took another hit.

For a moment, she had a taste of what it would be like to be the normal family that she always dreamed about with a mother and father and children.

It hurt.

Kelly caught April at the dessert table. "He cleans up well for church," she whispered.

"What?"

"Don't play dumb."

April watched as Joel talked to the pastor and David Baker, Kelly's husband. "I guess he's okay."

Kelly studied her friend as if she didn't understand the words coming out of her mouth. "You're either blind or kidding yourself. Why, every woman who has a child in Cora's class gushed about the dreamy cowboy who was checking in the two-year-olds. I would've known sooner, but I don't have any two-year-olds. Just three-, four-and six-year-olds and a soon-to-be newborn."

"Did you finally tell Dave?"

"I did, but you're not going to divert me. As I said, your ranch help cleans up well."

"He'll do."

"Oh, you have that denial thing *bad*." Kelly looked over April's shoulder at said cowboy.

"Okay, he's nice looking," April admitted.

"And he worked in the Sunday school class." Shaking her head, Kelly hooked arms with April and started toward Joel. "Why don't we join the conversation instead of hiding behind Wilma Olsen's potato salad?"

April knew she wouldn't hear the last of this for a long time.

Joel recognized an interrogation when he was at the wrong end of it. Pastor Terry Martin and Dave Baker sat across from him. The boys and Cora were at the other end of the long table, laughing and teasing with other children.

"So, what did you do before you were on the rodeo circuit?" the pastor asked.

"I ranched most of my life. My folks owned a ranch west of Fort Worth."

"And what made you leave it and travel with

the rodeo?" Dave asked as he took a bite of the cake April had brought.

He explained about his sister and her husband. "Once they married, they gave me the opportunity to follow my dream. It was a good excuse for me to leave the newlyweds alone. Gramps is still there, but I wanted to leave them alone while they worked out things the first year of married life."

The light seemed to go on in both men's heads.

"So you didn't have an itch to be away from your ranch?" the pastor asked.

He thought about it. "I probably wouldn't have tried my hand at the championship belt buckle again, but the doors all opened for me."

"And now?" Dave asked.

"Well, I'm in good shape to compete for that prize, but when the boys hired me for the week, I was glad to help April plant her fields."

The two men studied him.

Cora walked over to Joel. She raised her arms and he picked her up. Looking across the table, Joel said, "Miss Cora has me trained."

A silent message passed between the two men.

"Women are like that," Dave said. "No matter what our plans are, the ladies manage to change our direction."

Dave's comment lodged in Joel's heart like a cocklebur no matter how much he wanted to ignore it. As he looked down into Cora's precious face, the idea of having his own family—wife and babies—tugged at his heart again. And oddly enough, that family resembled the one he'd spent this past week with.

April grabbed an apple out of the bowl on her kitchen table and walked out to the fence. Spice stood there as if waiting for someone to notice her.

"Hello, pretty lady." April offered the horse an apple. "Have you enjoyed your time here on the ranch as much as my boys enjoyed having you and Joel here?"

Spice poked her head over the fence and took several bites of the apple. April stroked the horse's neck while Spice finished her treat. "I know Wes and Todd have loved these last few days, learning how to take care of the ranch and basking in the attention they've received." But what would they do when Joel left?

That dilemma had kept her up last night. Joel had been so good to the boys. Listened to them, taught them how to care for the ranch and showed them how to keep up the equipment.

He hadn't ignored them or made the boys feel as if they were imposing on him.

And Cora adored Joel.

April didn't want to examine her feelings for the man. Spice nudged her with her muzzle. "I don't have anything else, girl." April stroked the horse's neck. Spice reveled in the attention. "And I'm sure he takes good care of you, too, doesn't he?"

Today had taken on a dreamlike quality. Her boys had showed Joel around like a new toy they'd brought for show-and-tell. And when they got home this afternoon after the lunch, Joel had gone to the barn and fixed a couple of bridles that needed repair. She hadn't said anything to him, but the man observed things that needed to be done and did them without anyone asking or prompting him to do so. She still couldn't overcome her awe of the man. He didn't need to be prodded or directed. He saw a need and worked until it was fixed.

Spice stuck her head beside her.

"So tell me, girl, what do you think of him? It certainly would be helpful if you could voice an opinion."

Without Spice's input, she'd just have to make her own judgment. But at this point, she didn't know what that was.

"So, does Joel take as good care of you as he has the things around here?"

"I hope I do." Joel's deep voice came from the gathering darkness.

April's heart jumped into her throat. How a man his size moved so quietly, she didn't know. "I'm sure you do, but I thought I'd go straight to the horse's mouth."

He laughed and she realized what she'd just said. "And has Spice spilled the beans?"

"She just looks content." She refused to look at him. "I hope you didn't mind the grilling you got this afternoon."

He shrugged. "It just shows that your friends and fellow church members care about you."

"The first time my in-laws took me to church, I found a home."

"What about your husband?"

She looked at the ground. "I noticed Ross's reaction to church but chose to ignore it. I told myself surely I was wrong. I wasn't."

He didn't ask any further questions, for which she was thankful. It had been painfully obvious Ross wasn't interested in church. He'd found so many excuses to avoid going with them on Sundays. She should've known something was wrong, but in the first flush of love, she'd conveniently ignored those little warnings. It didn't matter, she'd told herself.

It did.

Ross had only gone with them because his parents expected it, but she didn't doubt when Ross was away on a job, he'd never seen the inside of a church or opened a Bible.

Joel reached out and stroked Spice. "I love the evenings out here in the Panhandle. I didn't realize how mild the nights are during the summer. At home, we can't catch a break after dark, when it still remains hot after the sun goes down, but I could learn to love this."

Like musical notes, his words lifted her soul. "Then why are you on the circuit if you love ranch life so much? It seems inconsistent."

She sounded like a jerk after his wonderful rendition of spring.

His hand closed over hers. "It seems contradictory, doesn't it?"

She couldn't concentrate on what he said. Her mind focused on where his hand surrounded hers. As hard as she tried to understand, her brain had gone on overload. "Uh, yes."

His gaze locked with hers and he slowly lowered his head toward her.

The screen door slammed, bursting the bubble surrounding them. The boys stood on the porch.

"Could you come inside and say good-night, Mr. Joel, before you leave?"

Saved by a screen door. Her heart beat so hard she thought it would jump out of her chest.

His gaze didn't move from her face for several moments. He broke the connection and looked at the boys. "Of course I'll come in and say goodnight." He leaned down and whispered, "I'll be back."

April watched as her boys waited on Joel. It stole her breath. They were so eager to have a man's time and attention. And what would the boys do when Joel was gone? Would they pay the price?

And she had allowed it.

"So what are you going to do tomorrow?" Wes asked as he settled into bed.

"We're going to get ready for the rodeo. It takes a lot of work." Joel sat at the end of Wes's bed.

"Will you be able to come see us?" Todd asked. He pulled his arms out from under the covers.

"I don't think I'll be able to come out here, but you two and your sister and mom will get to see the different events on Friday and Saturday. That's when all the excitement and fun happens. And when you come, I expect you to bring your lariats and show me your progress."

The boys sat up and nodded their heads.

"I'll practice every day after school," Wes replied.

"Me, too," Todd promised, lying back down. His face clouded over. "I wish we had another week of vacation."

Joel pulled the covers up to his chin. "I'll hold you to that promise, because it will show up in your skill on Friday if you've practiced every day."

Todd picked at his sheet.

Resting his palm on Todd's head, Joel smiled at the little boy.

Wes scooted under his covers. "We'll miss you."

Joel's heart skipped a beat. "Well, boys, you should be proud of yourselves since you helped your mother. I know she's proud of you. And I'm honored to have worked for you."

The mood in the room turned solemn.

"I look forward to seeing you on Friday." Joel winked.

Todd smiled, but it was the saddest smile Joel had ever witnessed on a young boy. With a final good-night, Joel turned off the light and walked out of the room.

Joel's mood darkened as he walked outside. He wanted to help April and her family with the ranch and catching up on work around the property, but seeing the sadness in the boys' faces, Joel didn't know if he'd done the family any favors.

When Joel walked out of the house, the teasing romantic attitude he'd gone in with had evaporated, putting a damper on April's giddiness. What had happened? Had the children said something? Had he responded back? The protective mother bear in her rose up.

"Is everything all right?"

"Fine." His tone called him a liar.

After several moments of silence, he said,

"I'll load Spice in the trailer and head back to the rodeo."

The dreamy quality of the night evaporated as she slapped up against reality. She should be grateful he seemed so distant, because if things had continued on the road they were on, disaster would've been the only possible ending for them.

"There's lots of work to get ready for the rodeo. I won't be out here this week, but if you have a problem, just call." He walked to his horse trailer, retrieved his rope and peppermints.

"Spice," he called.

The horse raised her head and trotted to where he stood. Unwrapping the candy, he offered it to the mare while he slipped the halter over her head, snapped on the lead rope and led her out of the paddock to the trailer. This time, the horse didn't hesitate. After securing the doors on the trailer, he climbed into the driver's seat. "I'll look forward to seeing y'all on Friday." With a final nod he drove away.

As she watched him disappear down the drive, she told herself it was just the fallout with the kids that unsettled her. That was all it could be. Nothing personal.

Somehow she couldn't swallow that explanation.

Once back at the auditorium, Joel went on autopilot, unloading Spice and putting her in the corral with the other horses. He pitched in and helped with evening chores.

"So you decided to show up," Shortie McGraw teased. "We were thinking that you might not want to come back to the rodeo after spending time on that ranch."

"I was working. I went to church this morning. Did you?"

Shortie blushed. "Well, Charlie Newman wasn't here. So what gopher hole did you step in to make you so cranky?"

Joel couldn't fault the man. But keeping Shortie diverted benefited Joel. He didn't want to talk about his time with April and the kids. Joel hauled back on his emotions. Shortie didn't mean anything. The men around them all stopped and looked at them.

"Sorry, Shortie. I didn't mean to snap."

"No problem."

But it was. Joel hadn't realized it would hurt so much to leave the family. The look in the boys' eyes had cut straight across his heart, making it nearly impossible to walk out of their bedroom and out of the house, and after next weekend, out of their lives.

When he'd gone back outside and seen April with her soft smile and sparkling eyes, he'd known he'd skated too close to an edge that neither he nor April were ready to fall over. Helping this week was the deal he'd made with the boys. That was all. Nothing more.

Other cowboys showed up from their time away from the rodeo and unloaded their horses. As they joined in, the talk turned away from Joel's week to the jobs that needed to be done. The facilities manager and his employees would work with Jack and some of the cowboys to help with the setup.

After all the animals were fed, several of the cowboys drifted over to the concession area for coffee and anything sweet that Hank had on hand.

Joel didn't feel like shooting the breeze.

"Hey, Kaye, you coming with us?" Shortie asked.

"Naw, it's been a long day, and I think I did all my socializing with the church crowd this morning." Joel didn't have enough energy left in him to keep a running volley with the other guys.

"I understand."

Joel walked back to his trailer and hooked it up to the electricity outlet. He opened the door to the front compartment, where there was a bed, a tiny closet and a dresser. This had become his home. He could easily touch each side of the compartment. How Caleb had lived in this space for more than ten years Joel would never know. If he wanted running water for a shower or bathroom facilities he had to find a truck stop. At least here, the coliseum provided nice facilities for their contestants.

Hanging his cowboy hat on the hook on the door, he used the bootjack by the bed and took off his boots. He lay back on the bed ready to unwind when his phone rang. The first thought that popped into his head was something was wrong at the ranch.

"Hello."

"Hey, bro, how are you doing?" Brenda asked.

"Sis." It took a moment for him to realize there wasn't an emergency he'd have to deal with at April's ranch. "How's it going? Everything okay?" His heart sped up, worried something was wrong. "Gramps—"

"Everything's fine. How are things on the circuit?"

"Great."

"You sure? You sounded like you're ready to charge somewhere."

That bad? Joel needed to rein in his reactions if he didn't want every cowboy on the circuit making fun of his—

His what?

"I thought you might have been someone else."

Brenda didn't say anything for several moments. "Must be someone important."

"Just the rancher I helped out this week."

"I thought you were doing rodeo."

Sometimes his sister could drive him crazy.

"You called just to hassle me? Isn't your husband target enough?"

"Ah, that's the brother I know and love."

Her cheerful teasing made him smile. "What did you call about, brat?"

"And to think I pulled your bacon out of the fire by organizing that charity rodeo."

She'd come through by taking over the charity rodeo their church and other churches had given to help the financially strapped ranchers in their hometown and surrounding counties. That rodeo had put his sister on the right road for a career after she left the army, and she'd collected a husband to boot. "I owe you, sis."

She went silent. "I called with news."

"Oh, and what is that?"

"You're going to be an uncle."

Joel sat up. "Really?"

"That's what Caleb's reaction was, too. Do you think I go around pulling jokes about being pregnant? None of the men under my command thought I had a sense of humor."

"It's just such good news." He felt himself grinning. "So how's your husband?"

"He's gone weird. You'd think I couldn't walk across the room without his help."

"Not true," he heard Caleb yell.

"It is, but I find it charming."

Joel snorted. He asked about the due date and

other important information about the newest member of the family. "How's Gramps taking it?"

"He's loving it. Another generation of Kayes— well, sort of. He's wondering when you're going to get with the program."

"I didn't say that," he heard Gramps complain.

"I'd hoped you would've come home while there was a break in the rodeo schedule, but that didn't happen."

"Well, there was a rancher around here who hired me to help with planting."

"A rancher?"

The way his sister said *rancher* made him squirm. "Yes, a rancher."

"You could've come home and helped Caleb with our fields."

"The circumstances were unusual and I was needed here."

The line remained quiet. Finally she said, "I'm glad you're keeping your hand in ranching. Someday I'd like to meet this rancher."

He didn't doubt it for a minute. "Someday you might."

"Sounds like a plan."

He needed to steer this conversation in a different direction. "So are you going to continue on with your counseling certification?"

"I am. I'm only pregnant, not crippled."

Caleb and he needed to walk a fine line between being concerned and letting her do her thing. Brenda had achieved the rank of captain in the army and was used to ordering folks around. At least with him being out on the rodeo circuit he wouldn't have to worry too much about dealing with her on a daily basis. "Thanks for calling, sis."

After he hung up, Joel's mind raced over the conversation again. Brenda had sounded joyful and excited. Full of life, literally and figuratively. He didn't begrudge her that happiness. It had been a long, hard road for her, but she'd made it.

Taking a deep breath, he listened to the muted sounds of the cowboys talking. He could open the door and join the others in seeing who could spin the largest story, but he'd still feel alone, and when he came back to the trailer, he'd still be alone.

The time with April and her children had touched him in a way he hadn't expected. He'd had eager young minds looking to him and a baby girl who sought shelter in his arms every time she was near him. Just remembering warmed him, making him feel ten feet tall. He now understood why his father would stand out on the porch in the evening, surveying the land as far as he could see, and smile, saying life couldn't be sweeter.

But it was the strong woman whose smile made his heart ache and want more that haunted him the most. He didn't want to confess to his sister that the rancher was a woman. He wasn't ready to talk about his week before he could wrestle it down.

If he kept on the pace he was on now, winning in the summer and throughout the fall, adding points to his total, he'd be in the finals in Las Vegas again. When he went back out on the circuit, it had just been a dream, and now it was looking mighty good for a win.

But with his sister's announcement she was pregnant, he suddenly had an ache for babies of his own.

He slipped under the covers and tried to go to sleep. He might as well have tried to wrestle down every bull the rodeo had—it wasn't happening.

When he closed his eyes, he saw April smiling at him, as she had earlier in the evening. The look in her eyes had said *stay*. But he knew that stay came with a price—no more rodeo.

That couldn't be. He'd lost this dream once before, and although he didn't resent going home to help care for the ranch and be with his sister her senior year in high school, it left some unfinished business hanging over his head, which he'd like to finish this time.

Chapter Nine

"C'mon, boys, the bus should be out on the road in a few minutes."

The boys dragged out of their bedroom. The first day after vacation was always hard, but today seemed particularly bad especially after the whirlwind week they'd had. Their faces were so long, April was surprised the boys didn't fall over them. She gave each boy his backpack and lunch pack.

"Thanks, Mom," Todd replied.

Wes simply grunted.

She opened the back door and shooed them outside. Scooping up Cora, April followed the boys down the drive to her mailbox. Before they got to the end of the drive, the bus stopped.

"Hurry, boys," she encouraged.

The bus driver opened the door and waved at April. "Did you have a good vacation?" the driver called out.

"We did. You?"

"Went to Galveston."

"We got tickets to the rodeo," Wes told the bus driver as he passed her. "And it was so exciting to have Mr. Joel here."

"Mr. Joel?" The driver threw April a puzzled look.

As if a switch had been thrown, her two draggy sons found their voices going from sluggish and depressed to excited and bragging, which startled her.

"No, let me tell her," Todd said as he stepped on the bus. "He's with the rodeo but helped us all vacation."

The driver's eyes widened. "Our drive to school will be interesting. See you this afternoon." She closed the door and drove off.

April realized that by the time the boys got home, everyone in the school and probably for twenty miles around would know about Joel Kaye. She'd better be ready to talk.

It didn't take until the kids came home. By eleven-thirty, she'd gotten five calls. When the school secretary called, April knew the boys had been working overtime.

"Are you getting married?" Sandra Grayson asked.

April nearly dropped the phone. "No. Why would you ask?"

"Well, the way Todd and Wes were talking, I expected to attend your wedding this weekend."

Scrambling to come up with an answer, April took a deep breath. "We're going to the rodeo this weekend. That's all."

"Really?"

"I promise, Sandra."

"So there's no Mr. Joel you're marrying?"

There it was. "Uh, there is a Joel Kaye who works for the rodeo. He picked up some horses last week, but there's no marriage in sight."

"The boys talked about how they hired him to help at your place. So that's not true?"

"Well, that's true. After Mr. Moore got hurt last week, the boys came up with the idea of hiring Joel to help out with the planting and chores."

"And you're not getting married?"

Oddly enough, April wanted to cry. "I assure you, Sandra, Joel only helped me plant my hay and sunflowers. My sons have a promising career in writing fiction if they don't want to continue to ranch."

Sandra laughed. "I understand. My daughter told all the neighbors that her parents were getting divorced. We were discussing my cousin's problems. I had to field a lot of calls from my family. I'll put the kibosh on the rumors here at school."

"Thanks, Sandra."

After April hung up, she called Kelly. "I'm going to need your help."

"What's wrong?"

"Well, apparently my sons are talking about Joel being here last week, and somehow it's morphed into me getting married to Joel this weekend."

"That's a good idea."

April blinked, wondering when she'd fallen down the rabbit hole.

"You there?"

April didn't know how long she'd been silent. "Yes." She sounded as though she'd swallowed a frog.

"I was only teasing."

The sounds of Cora playing with her horse and dolls in her room drifted into the kitchen. "Am I so pathetic that you think I need to get married?"

"Oh, sweetie, I didn't mean to upset you. You've held up under what would've crushed most of us. It's not about whether or not you can do it all, but it's about you having someone to help and support you."

"The Lord provides."

"And you can count on Him, but sometimes He sends us help in the form of people—or in this case a cowboy. Joel could fit that bill."

Kelly's words robbed April of breath. "I might be wrong, Kelly, but I don't need another man who has an itch to move from town to town. I had enough of that growing up with my dad. Then I managed to marry a man just like my father."

"Maybe Joel isn't the one, but don't close your heart, April. You might be missing what God sends your way."

Deep inside, April knew that Kelly had a point. "Okay, I'll relax, but I'm not expecting too much."

"That, my friend, is your problem."

Hanging up the phone, April walked down to her daughter's room and stood out in the hall, listening to her play with her horsey. She made whinnying sounds, then her voice lowered. "Sugar, come here."

From her daughter's conversation, a cowboy called his horse. April didn't doubt Cora's conversation imitated Joel's with his horse.

Leaning her head back on the wall, April closed her eyes. Tears slid down both cheeks. The time Joel had been here had been a joy.

She wondered what she would've done if Joel had tried to kiss her when he'd come out to talk to her last night. Thankfully, her boys had interrupted the moment. She had no business kissing Joel. It would only bring trouble.

Trouble she didn't need.

"Why don't we take a break, Joel? You're going to give me a heart attack," Jack complained as they finished the chutes for the bulls. "We don't need to finish everything this morning. I could use a cup of coffee."

Yesterday, the guys had just shot the breeze as they started to set up things for the rodeo. There was no hurry or rush to get things done, since the setup didn't need to be finished until Wednesday. The cowboys planned to teach a one-day workshop for high-school students, evaluating them and helping with the events they participated in.

This morning, Joel was determined to work until he dropped so he wouldn't have to think. But from the look in Jack's eyes, Joel knew the older man needed a break.

"Sounds good."

Joel followed his friend to the concession area.

"Hank, we need a couple cups of coffee," Jack called out.

They sat down at a picnic table.

"Had I known sending you out to work on a ranch would've produced such a firestorm, I would've sent you sooner. Maybe I need the other guys to work on the ranches around the cities where we stop."

"I'd like to see that, Jack."

Hank showed up with the cups of coffee and placed them in front of each man.

"I just thought I'd get the setup done after the time off," Joel continued. "Yesterday not too much got done, so I thought we needed to get in gear today for that workshop tomorrow."

Both Hank and Jack studied him.

"I admire an industrious cowboy, but you seemed a bit more motivated this morning." Jack took a sip of his coffee.

Joel hadn't slept much over the past two nights, wrestling with the memories of April and her children. His sister's news hadn't helped the situation. He cheered for her and Caleb, but their good news only pointed out how alone he was. It put an ache in his heart for— He stopped the thought cold. "Well, I thought we wanted the facility done before those elementary schoolers came by to see the rodeo."

"What are you talking about?" Jack asked.

Grasping on to any excuse he could, Joel explained, "I heard a couple of ladies in the front office this morning after breakfast talking about the elementary kids coming out here today on some sort of field trip. Is that true?"

"That's right. I forgot." Jack took a deep draw of his coffee. "The school district, auditorium managers and our boss came up with a plan, then notified me Monday morning. I wish they'd notified me last week. I'm going to check in with the front office." He finished off his coffee and left.

"So we'll have little ones running around here until the rodeo," Hank commented.

"Appears so."

"Since I didn't see you for several days, I assume you were fed."

"There are others who are willing to feed a cowboy."

"And those others wouldn't be a nice-looking widow woman?"

"It was."

"She's got some cute kids."

"True."

"Am I going to have to pull teeth?"

Hank knew how to make a cowboy smile. "She's got great kids. I'm glad I was able to help her."

"That's a good thing."

Hank started away, much to Joel's surprise.

"You're not going to give me a hard time about April?"

"Naw, you're going to get enough from everyone else. I'll spare you."

Hank's answer puzzled him.

Jack appeared. "It seems we've got several tours later today and a couple of tours tomorrow besides the high-school students we expected. Let's finish setting up."

April and Kelly ended up being the parent volunteers who accompanied the children on the field trip from the elementary school to the rodeo. Or, rather, Kelly called April the night before to inform her she'd volunteered April to help her chaperone. Kelly had also arranged for her mother-in-law to take care of Cora's and Kelly's younger kids.

Both Todd and Wes beamed with pride after telling their classmates they'd already been to the rodeo, walked around and met some of the cowboys. And they knew a special cowboy.

The head teacher who organized the field trip directed the kids to the front office.

Jack Murphy met the group, introducing himself. "It's nice to see you again, Mrs. Landers."

"Please call me April. *Mrs. Landers* makes me feel like my mother-in-law."

The tour began with Jack explaining to the kids how they set up the rodeo in each city visited.

When they moved to where the horses were corralled, Wes and Todd pointed out Sadie and Helo.

"Those are the horses my grandpa raised," Wes said to his classmates.

The kids oohed and aahed, gathering around the boys.

"It appears you have stars," Kelly whispered to April.

"Who knew?" Seeing her boys bask in their classmates' admiration made April smile.

"Mr. Joel," Todd called out. He waved at Joel, who was walking toward the tour group.

April looked in the direction of Todd's greeting. Joel.

Her heart sped up despite her promise to herself to remain cool.

"He's a mighty fine-looking man, in case you didn't notice that before," Kelly whispered.

April glared at her friend. Kelly grinned unrepentantly.

"Well, Todd," Joel's voice rang out, "what are you doing here?"

"We're on a tour of the rodeo." Todd introduced Joel to all his classmates and teacher. The girls giggled, the boys shook Joel's hand and the teacher blushed. "He knows how to lasso horses and cows. And he helped us at the ranch last week."

Todd's classmates looked in awe from Todd to Joel.

Joel greeted the adults. "Mrs. Landers, Mrs. Baker."

"Joel, I thought we were on a first-name basis," Kelly replied.

April had thought so, too.

"My mama taught me to wait for permission before calling a person by their first name." He shrugged.

The teacher turned to the first and third graders. "Do you see the proper way to address people? This cowboy has it right."

The children nodded in amazement. Joel won the respect of every child there.

They proceeded with Jack explaining what the cowboys did and how they cared for the animals.

April tried to ignore Joel walking beside her, but his presence blotted out any clear thinking.

They paused at the concession stand, where Hank served cartons of milk and cookies.

Joel started to leave, but Wes caught him. "Would you sit with us and have cookies and milk?"

April held her breath.

"Sure."

The tension drained out of her. April purposely sat at a different table from Joel.

"What are you doing?" Kelly demanded.

"I'm sitting with the kids, supervising them."

"Why aren't you sitting with your son?"

"Because his teacher is at that table."

Kelly growled under her breath. "You need to say hello to Joel before we leave."

"This isn't a date for me. I'm the chaperone."

"Sometimes I wonder if you know how to have fun."

"I do."

"Then show it," Kelly hissed, then walked to the table where Joel sat.

After Kelly chatted with Joel, he looked at April and smiled. She tried to keep control of her heart, but that organ didn't pay any attention to her head.

"Okay, children, it's time to go back to school.

We need to thank all the people from the rodeo who have shown us what they do."

A chorus of thank-yous rang out in the auditorium.

April stood and ushered all her charges back to the front door. Looking ahead, she saw Wes and Todd hurry toward Joel and exchange words.

"It's neat to meet a real rodeo cowboy." Ashley Summer, a girl in Wes's class, sighed.

"Your dad's a cowboy," April replied.

Ashley did a double take. "My father's old, and he's my father." She paused. "He's okay, but—" She shook her head.

April bit her lip. "I guess you're right."

Shaking her head, Ashley whispered to her friend.

They filed outside. Jack and Joel helped the kids back onto the bus. As the line shrank, April found herself slowly approaching Joel. He helped the girls up the steps, which brought giggles and blushes.

The boys gave Joel a nod or shook his hand. When she and the teacher were the last ones left to board, Joel offered April his hand.

"Where's Cora?"

"She's with Kelly's mother-in-law with her two younger children." She wanted to smile at him like the schoolgirls before her, but felt silly.

The teacher behind her cleared her throat, causing April to step up onto the first step. Joel wrapped his hand around her forearm to steady her and had his hand on her back for extra support. April pulled herself up the last step and found a seat in the first row. Joel repeated his action with the teacher, helping her on the bus.

The teacher, a single woman in her late twenties, flashed him an inviting smile.

Joel's actions were simply that of a polite cowboy helping two women onto the bus, she told herself. He didn't step back but continued to look at April. Her son's teacher gave her a strange look.

"I'll look forward to seeing your family on Friday. Bring them early. I think Spice, Sadie and Helo might enjoy seeing the boys and Cora again."

"We'll do that."

He nodded and stepped away.

April didn't doubt her little exchange with Joel would be broadcast all over the school, generating more calls.

The school grapevine should be funny. It wasn't.

Kelly drove back from the elementary school to her mother-in-law's house, where April had left her car.

"It's truly amazing that of all the cowboys that could've come to your ranch and picked up those horses, it was Joel that showed up. You've been praying for help, haven't you?" Kelly asked.

"Of course I've been praying for help."

"And did you ask for a tall, good-looking cowboy?"

April rolled her eyes. "Pastor would set you straight on how to pray. God knows your needs. I prayed for help out of my situation." Suddenly, April heard the words that came out of her mouth. She clamped her mouth shut.

Kelly's glance nailed April. After a moment of silence, Kelly started talking about her husband's reaction to her pregnancy. "You'd think this was my first."

April's mind drifted to seeing Joel. Her heart certainly rebelled against any logic, no matter how her head knew a rodeo cowboy was a man with an itch to wander, but that was not what her heart was saying.

How could that be?

"Dave's been great to bring me home romaine lettuce and Caesar dressing. I think I just may have him bring me home the anchovies and eat them straight out of the can."

April shivered. "Ick."

"Didn't you have any cravings when you were pregnant?"

A dart of sadness struck her heart. She wouldn't have any more babies. She shook it off. "Food, but anchovies—you'll probably have to eat them yourself. I don't see your rancher husband loving them."

"He's okay with them on the pizza."

"Yeah, he's okay with them 'cause he has to be, but if he went out with other ranchers to Fort Worth to look for stock, I doubt he'd order them."

"True."

"You know, you've got a keeper there. Not too many of the ranchers around here would go for anchovies. You don't want him drummed out of the cowboy club."

Throwing her head back, Kelly laughed. "For sure. I don't think David told his parents, either."

Parking in the driveway of her mother-in-law's house, Kelly turned off the engine. "I have your word you'll keep my husband's secret?"

"It's safe with me."

After picking Cora up, April drove home. She couldn't help but smile at the thought of David Baker having to hide his love of a certain kind of pizza. Whoever would've thought a rancher like David loved anchovies? Maybe sausage or pepperoni—but then again, who would've thought her own husband would refuse to go near a steer or heifer after he grew up?

She wondered what Joel liked on his pizza.

Stop. Don't go there. Only trouble lies in that direction.

Still, she couldn't help herself.

There were still a few cowboys sitting at the table after the evening meal.

"I'll be glad when the rodeo starts tomorrow. I'm looking forward to competing," Shortie McGraw said. "Are you going to be able to stay on that horse tomorrow, Joel, to win some more points?" The rest of the guys at the table went quiet.

"That's the idea."

"Those old bones of yours goin' to hold up?" The teasing tone of Shortie's words let the others know the younger man simply was pressing Joel's buttons.

"It seems to me I wasn't the one who dislocated his shoulder when I got tossed off Rumble," Joel drawled.

"He's got you there, Shortie. 'Course, Rumble has managed to get most of the guys on the circuit," Ty added. "When he threw me, I couldn't sit for a couple of days."

"That horse broke Adam's ribs."

Rumble's name had been well earned.

"You didn't answer my question," Shortie pressed.

"If I didn't plan on staying on a bucking horse, I wouldn't be here."

The other cowboys grinned and chuckled. After another couple of rounds of comments and laughs, the group broke up, and Joel walked over to the corral housing Spice. The horse whinnied and nodded her head in greeting.

"You ready to get to work tomorrow, girl?"

Spice nosed Joel's hand, wanting to be petted.

"Along with working, you'll see a couple of boys who think you're extra special—not that you're not."

Spice wandered off, leaving Joel standing at the fence.

"Don't let Shortie's mouth bother you." Jack came to a stop beside Joel.

"It didn't. Just youthful boasts."

"So you're out here talking to the horses 'cause talking to your fellow cowboys is worse?" Jack's brow arched.

"I hadn't thought of it that way. Sounds kinda bad."

"Well, there are moments I'm tempted to agree with you."

"When my parents and grandmother died, I found myself talking a lot to my horse. If anyone would've heard me, they'd have thought me a nutcase, but lots of problems got worked out. Lately, folks are finding out how healing riding and caring for horses can be. Brenda rode to build up her strength after her time in the hospital." He sighed. "I'm not interested in shooting the breeze and playing mind games with my fellow contestants." That made him feel old. Oddly, working all day on the ranch didn't.

"I hear you. Guess that's part of growing up, being confident about your talent. But if you keep winning and gaining points, you can show those younger cowboys how wrong they are. I'm going to be cheering for you. Those youngsters need to know that older cowboys have class and finesse and technique, which compensates for brute strength."

"How old were you when you won your buckle?"

"The first one, twenty-six. The second at thirty-two."

"So there's hope for me." Jack's answer gave Joel something to hold on to.

"Yeah, but I will own up to it being harder the second time."

As Joel walked back to his trailer, he felt less like a crotchety old man. Once settled under the sheets in bed, he realized what he actually missed was the unpredictable questions he got from two little boys.

He shook his head. What was going on?

Chapter Ten

The boys vibrated with excitement when they got off the bus on Friday afternoon. April hadn't ever seen them sprint up the drive that fast before. Both boys were out of breath when they ran inside.

"We're here, Mom," Wes called out. "I want to change into my boots before we go, but I'll be fast."

Todd didn't say anything but pulled off his running shoes as he made his way to his room.

"Don't leave your shoes in the hall."

Todd didn't object but simply picked up his shoes and ran into his room.

By the time April had Cora's stroller in the truck and her buckled into her car seat, the boys had appeared. Each one had his lasso with him. It took only moments to buckle everyone in.

"Hurry up, Mom, and get in. We want to go," Wes encouraged her.

Talk about the shoe being on the other foot. They were focused on leaving for the rodeo and nothing else.

"How was your day?" she asked as she drove.

"Lots of kids are coming tonight. They asked about Mr. Joel and if he was going to compete," Todd answered. "I told them yes."

"Dale told me his brother is in the steer wrestling and his big sister will do barrel racing tonight."

As the boys talked, April smiled at the animation and excitement in their voices. It seemed the Lord had dropped Joel into their lives to restore their youthful enthusiasm. Last year when their grandfather took them to the rodeo, it had been shortly after their grandmother's death. They'd enjoyed themselves, but it was nothing compared to this year.

Much to her embarrassment, she shared her children's excitement. She was a grown woman, but her tingly spine and dancing stomach didn't think she was too old for such silliness. Next they would do a jig.

Turning off the road at the auditorium drive, the truck bounced with the boys' excitement. Their attitude rubbed off on Cora. "Yeah, we here."

Only a few trucks dotted the parking lot, giving April her choice. Pulling close to the front door, she parked and hurriedly unbuckled Cora and Todd. Wes stood by the front of the truck waiting for them, like a horse being held back from a race. Once she locked the truck, Wes rushed ahead of them to the glass doors and managed to open one. He waved them forward.

One of the women behind the glass ticket counter signaled them to come inside.

"Mr. Joel said we should come early," Todd announced. "Mom—" he pointed over his shoulder "—has the tickets."

Before April could scold her son, the woman nodded. "I know. Go back to the concession area and Hank will find Joel for you."

At least they were known.

As they walked to the concession area, other cowboys saw them and waved. Both boys returned the greetings, reveling in the attention.

"Hey, Ty," Wes called out.

He returned the greeting. "Are you going to show us how you've been practicing with your lariats?" Ty finished his cookie.

"I am," Wes answered.

"Mr. Hank," Todd called out, "we're here. I can't wait to see all the cowboys compete."

"The lady at the front said you'd find Mr. Joel for us," Wes said.

Cora climbed up onto the picnic bench. She looked at Hank and smiled. The older man smiled back.

Todd scanned the area. "Are you going to get Mr. Joel?"

"He's been told you're here."

Todd didn't look convinced until Joel walked into the area several moments later. April's stomach started dancing again.

"Mr. Joel," the boys cried, racing toward him, each grabbing a leg.

After greeting Todd and Wes, Joel squatted in front of Cora. "How's my girl today?"

"'Cited." She raised her arms.

Without any hesitation, Joel scooped her up. He turned to April. "I'm glad you're here." The tone of his voice changed, softening and making her think it was more than just a greeting. Something more intimate.

She swallowed. "Wild horses wouldn't have kept the boys away."

"And you?"

He'd nailed her. She felt heat run up her neck. Her feelings were all over the map, bringing lots of complications, but they were there. "Me, too," she whispered.

He leaned closer to hear her, bringing his face inches from hers.

She wanted to ask if he'd missed them, but the boys tugged on his shirt.

"Can we see Spice?"

"Well, I hoped you'd get here early enough to help me with getting Spice brushed and saddled before she starts working. Spice likes a little attention before the night's competition. And we have to brush her after, too."

Wes frowned. "That's a lot."

"It's part of taking care of your mount. Spice works hard for me out there in the arena. I have to take care of her."

A good lesson Wes and Todd needed to learn and see put into action. How could she ever repay Joel for the lessons he'd taught so naturally to the kids?

"Besides," he added, "just like every other woman, Spice likes to look nice."

April arched her brow. "Because she's a woman?"

Joel simply grinned.

She wanted to laugh, again. This past week she'd felt free enough to throw her head back and laugh, and what a joy it had been.

They followed Joel to the section of the auditorium set up for grooming the horses. Called greetings followed the boys, and Wes and Todd acted like stars, with their chests puffed out, striding across the floor with purpose.

"They're looking like the genuine thing," Millie commented, laughter in her voice.

"As much as I try to raise them right, it takes a stranger to bring that spring to their steps." April glanced at Millie.

"Naw, it isn't a stranger—it's a cowboy thing. Something they want to be."

Was that it? Was it just the cowboy thing or was it *this* particular cowboy who spent time with her boys, taught them and made them laugh? Was it this particular cowboy that made her smile and laugh?

The question stuck with April as she watched the boys and Cora help groom Spice and saddle her. By the time they finished, the auditorium began to fill with spectators.

"I hungry," Cora announced, her voice carrying over the entire grooming area.

April wanted to melt into the floor.

"Me, too," Todd seconded.

"Well, we can't have hungry little cowboys and cowgirls. Let's go see Hank. You think hot dogs would help?" Joel grinned at the children.

Nods and yeses answered Joel's question.

Not having a choice, they went back to the concession area.

After ordering for the boys and Cora, Joel turned to her. "Want anything?"

"Well, if I'm going to be at the rodeo, might as well have a hot dog, too."

The twinkle in his eyes and the crook at the corner of his mouth made April feel as though she was living the dream of every high-school girl in this part of Texas—a handsome cowboy buying her dinner at the rodeo. Never mind it was a hot dog.

But this wasn't a date, she reminded herself, and she needed to buy her children their dinner.

April settled the kids at a table while Joel waited in line for their food.

"You stay here while I help Mr. Joel," April instructed the kids.

Joining Joel at the counter, she pulled out her wallet. "Here's money for the hot dogs."

He stared down at the money in her hand as if it was a snake. "Are we going back to square one? I thought we were friends. This is something I want to do for you and your children." His expression told her how ungracious she sounded.

"Thank you."

He nodded at her acceptance.

"You need any help carrying things?"

"That I could use." He handed her a couple of drinks while Hank piled the tray with the rest of the order.

Walking beside Joel to the table, she experienced again that feeling—that they were a real family with a mom, dad and kids. What was wrong with her? She knew better than to spin daydreams, because that was what they were— dreams. Not real, and when the dream evaporated, she'd have nothing left but sadness.

Looking at the table where the kids were, she saw Ty Newsome seated next to Wes.

"I've practiced," Wes told Ty, "and I can twirl."

"One time." Todd held up his index finger.

"One more time than you," Wes shot back.

"Keep working at it, boys." Ty looked up. "So you've taken up being a waiter, Joel?"

"Nope. Just a polite cowboy helping a fine lady carry her meal." Joel set the tray down. "Ty had a good idea, boys. If you practice twirling your lassoes, keeping them over your head, and help each other, you could be known as the twirling Landers Boys."

"Great idea," Ty added. "Next year you could come and show the audience what you can do."

Todd and Wes stilled, looked at each other and smiled.

Joel passed out hot dogs. When he handed April hers, he said, "I think your boys will come up with a plan."

When she turned her head, her lips nearly brushed his. His eyes darkened.

Someone cleared his throat, breaking the atmosphere.

Ty stood. "See you later, boys. Hope y'all will cheer for me in the saddle-bronc riding." He dipped his hat and walked away.

Joel finished passing out chips and drinks to the kids. April grabbed Cora's milk carton and opened it, focusing on the spout, trying to get control of her pounding heart.

Joel reached around her and pilfered the bag of

chips in front of the little girl and opened them, then returned the chips.

April could smell Joel's scent—a mixture of sweat and horse—and feel the heat of his body. She swallowed and looked at the area before him on the table.

"Didn't you get yourself anything to eat?" April asked.

"I don't eat before competing. After I finish, I'll chow down."

Wes frowned. "Chow down?"

"That means I'll eat a lot of food."

"Oh."

April stared down at her hot dog, struggling with all her conflicting emotions. She heard Cora giggle, then a crash. All conversation in the snack area stopped. When April looked up, Todd stood by the condiment barrel holding the spoon that had been in the relish crock. At his feet lay broken pottery. His eyes were huge.

"I wanted some more relish, Mama." His voice quivered. "I didn't mean to break it."

April stood and hurried toward Todd.

"I didn't mean to break it," he repeated.

"Oh, honey, I know you didn't."

Pottery and relish dotted the floor. Hank appeared with a broom. "Hey, partner, it's okay."

Joel stepped to Todd's side, lifted him out of the gooey mess and put him a safe distance away.

Relish covered the right shoulder of Todd's

Western shirt, his face and hair. Relish had also dotted his jeans and boots. Todd looked at himself and then at his mom. Tears filled his eyes.

April cupped Todd's cheek. "It's all wash-and-wear. C'mon, let's go get you cleaned up."

Todd's shoulders eased.

April turned to Joel. "Would you watch Wes and Cora?"

"Sure. Go get Todd cleaned up and ready to watch the rodeo."

In the ladies' bathroom, April helped Todd unsnap his Western shirt and place it on the sink, then turned on the faucet and rinsed out his shirt. "Now let's get the stuff out of your hair."

Todd wasn't tall enough to accomplish the task, so April picked him up and held him around his waist.

Millie walked into the restroom with a new Western shirt and some fancy jeans. "Here, let me help." She put the new clothes down on the counter several sinks away and supported Todd's feet. "I have some things here for the young man to change into."

Todd had his head under the faucet for round two. April turned off the water and wrung out his hair.

The older woman stepped back, waiting and watching.

"Thank you for the help, Millie. Let's see if the clothes will fit."

Millie handed April a plastic bag. "This is for the clothes that need washing."

"You've faced this situation before?"

"Sure have. I've got kids and grandkids. I know you're always facing something unexpected. Even my granddaughters are now providing me with challenges. A skunk was the latest adventure with my youngest granddaughter."

April turned to Todd. "You see, it could've been worse."

Todd eyed the two women, obviously not convinced.

Millie left.

Over the next ten minutes Todd's hair was dried under the hand dryer and he changed into the new Western shirt and jeans.

All of the joy and excitement of the rodeo seemed to have drained out of her son. She didn't want him to lose the delight of the night.

"Accidents happen, but next time, ask for help."

"I will."

When they walked out of the bathroom, the first thing April saw was Joel holding Cora and talking to Wes. It didn't take much imagination to see him as their father. The thought stopped her cold and made her palms sweat.

The concessions area now teemed with fans here to see the rodeo.

"You're looking mighty good, young man." Hank stood there smiling at Todd.

The words snapped her out of her daydreaming.

"I'm better. I'm sorry, Mr. Hank."

"Don't worry. Are you still hungry?"

Todd shook his head.

After joining the others at the table, Joel asked Todd, "Everything good?"

"I'm okay," Todd answered.

"April," Kelly called and dragged her family to where April sat. The children greeted each other.

Kelly's daughter studied Todd. "I like your clothes. Where did you get them?"

A tense silence followed.

Finally Todd said, "You can get a girl's shirt from Ms. Millie over at the souvenir stand."

The announcer came on the PA system. "Welcome, ladies and gentlemen. The cowboys are itching to go and the bulls and horses are ready to test these cowboys. Get to your seats, 'cause we're fixin' to get this here rodeo started."

"That's my cue," Joel said. "My event, saddle-bronc riding, is the second on the list of events, and I need to get ready. You'll need to hurry to your seats. You'll want to see how they open the rodeo."

"We'll be watching," Wes said.

"I'll cheer, Mr. Joel," Todd called out.

Joel nodded to each boy. He picked Cora up. "Are you going to be rooting for me, too?"

Cora leaned forward and gave him a loud kiss on the cheek.

"That's a great encouragement. One of the best I've had." Turning to April, he smiled. "You think I could get one from your mother?"

The children looked from one adult to the other.

April gave him a kiss on the cheek. Drawing back, she heard him whisper, "It would've been better a little lower and to the left. And with a lot more enthusiasm."

April scooped Cora out of Joel's arms. "Be safe," she whispered.

Something connected between them, which shook her to the core but also warmed her heart.

He turned and walked off.

"C'mon, Mom, let's go to our seats."

She shook off the confusing feelings and followed the boys into the arena.

As Joel waited his turn to ride, he thought of April and the kids out there in the stands, waiting for him. No one else had been there for him, cheering him on. It warmed him.

"You ready to try to gain some points on me, old man?" Shortie teased. "You think you're going to be able to stay on Hercules?"

"That's my goal."

Shortie shook his head. "That horse is mighty good at tossing off cowboys. Not too many stay on him for the full eight seconds."

"That's why a cowboy gets good scores on such a contrary animal."

"Kind of a good combo—old ornery horse and old cowboy." Shortie wagged his eyebrows.

"Hercules is a smart horse, but I know his tricks and will be watching for them."

With a shrug of his shoulders, Shortie turned and walked to the chute where the horse he'd drawn stood.

Joel turned his attention on chute two, where Hercules stood.

"Ignore McGraw," Buck Graham said. "He's just trying to rattle you."

"I know. I've done my share of razzing my competition."

Joel slipped his glove on his right hand for protection and climbed up the slats of the chute and slid his boot over the back of the horse.

Hercules stood still, but Joel felt the horse readying himself for when the gate opened. He adjusted his hand on the hack rein and settled in for the ride. He nodded to the cowboy at the gate and it swung open. The horse shot out and started his bucking and twirling.

Knowing the horse's movements, Joel prepared himself for the dips and the hard-left cut the horse loved to do. Joel kept his arm in the air to get the most points he could out of the ride, and the horse tried his best to throw Joel off.

Eight seconds seemed like an eternity, but

finally the buzzer sounded and Joel's fingers released his death grip on the ropes.

The pickup rider maneuvered close enough so Joel could grab his waist and pull himself off the bucking horse and land on his feet. Hercules spun and kicked out. Joel jumped out of the way in the nick of time, feeling the breeze from the horse's hooves.

The crowd gasped.

"That was close," the announcer said over the PA. "You okay, cowboy?"

Taking off his hat, Joel waved to the crowd.

"The score for Joel Kaye's ride is eighty-seven, which puts him in the lead. Congratulations, cowboy."

Joel walked toward the gate that allowed contestants in and out of the arena.

"Good score," several of the cowboys called out.

Joel nodded his acknowledgment. Looking into the audience where he knew the boys sat, Joel located them and waved. They waved back. Grins split their faces. April's expression puzzled him. It wasn't a frown, neither was it a smile, and she didn't wave.

He found himself wanting her approval. He dipped his hat toward her. She returned the greeting, making him smile.

"You flirting with members of the audience?" Jack asked.

"I am. 'Course, I wouldn't say smiling at the boys would be considered flirting."

"True, if that's what I was talking about."

"That's all it was."

"Yeah, and pull my other leg, Joel."

His attempt to redirect Jack failed. "I've got a horse that needs to be saddled for the next event."

"Good excuse."

Joel didn't hang around to argue the point. He needed to think about the next event and not about a woman whose mysterious expression threw him off.

"Wow, that was quite an exchange between you and Joel."

April whipped around and found Kelly sitting next to her. When she'd gotten there, April didn't know. Had she been that involved with Joel?

"Joel waved back to the boys."

"Yes, he did. It was the look afterward directed at you that I was talking about."

"It wasn't anything." The denial fell flat.

Kelly picked up April's hand. "It's okay, friend, to enjoy a smile from a good-looking cowboy."

"No, it's not."

"Lighten up. You don't have to be a stick in the mud."

"Am I that bad?"

Kelly laughed. "Oh, honey, there aren't words."

April's eyes widened.

"I'm not saying you haven't had a reason to be serious, but for tonight, enjoy yourself. Just let a handsome cowboy smile at you and flirt."

"But—"

"I'm not asking you to run wild and toss caution to the wind, but relax and have fun. I think sometimes we need those moments of laughter. Didn't Solomon say, 'A merry heart maketh a cheerful countenance'?"

"Maketh?"

Kelly poked April. "I did my Bible memorization from the King James Version. My mom thought that was the only legitimate translation. But what it says is your heart shows up on your face. Enjoy tonight, if only for your boys' sake. They are laughing and smiling, and if they keep looking back at their mother and you look like a thundercloud, you'll dampen their fun."

The truth hit April hard. "You're right."

"You better know it." Kellie pointed a finger at April. "Now, paste a smile on your face and enjoy. You have my permission."

"You're just in the pregnancy mode where you want everyone to be happy."

"Your point?"

"The nesting instinct."

Kelly laughed and waved off her friend. "Promise to enjoy yourself."

"I promise."

"My job here is done." Kelly stood and walked back to her seat.

"What did Mrs. Baker want?" Wes asked, tearing his gaze away from the arena.

"She wanted me to smile."

"Huh?"

"I'm supposed to have fun."

"I agree."

She did, too, which scared her.

Chapter Eleven

Joel led Spice back to the area where he could unsaddle her and brush her down.

"You were so good," Todd called out as he ran toward Joel.

"You had the best score in the saddle-bronc riding and number three in the calf roping," Wes added, beaming with pride. "Were you scared when the horse almost got you?"

April came to a stop behind Todd. Cora snuggled in her arms, the little girl's head resting on her mother's shoulder.

"I was and that's why you have to be careful when competing in the rodeo," Joel warned.

Wes nodded solemnly. "I really like the calf roping. I guess if I want to be in the rodeo, I'll have to learn to throw a lariat," Wes added. "Spice was real good in staying still when you jumped off." Wes faced the horse. "You were a good girl."

Spice nodded her head, accepting the praise.

"Boys, it's time to go back home. Your sister is worn-out and I need to put her to bed."

"Aw, Mom. Do we have to?" Wes asked.

Todd echoed his brother.

April wanted the boys to enjoy the moment, but her baby needed to go home.

"April, why don't you let the boys stay with me while I finish up with Spice? They need to see how to care for the horse after she's worked. I could drive them home after we're finished."

Joel had neatly trapped her. How could she say no? Looking at the boys' faces, she couldn't deny them. "Okay."

You would've thought Christmas morning had arrived from the expressions on their faces.

"They can't stay too late."

"I won't keep them much longer. We'll just take care of Spice and then head on out to the ranch."

"Boys, I expect you to behave yourselves."

"Promise, Mom."

Cora had passed out by the time April got her home. April had just put Cora in her bed when she heard a truck outside.

The boys danced in. Joel followed them. He'd been good to his word.

"Boys, you need to get ready for bed." Neither boy argued with her, and went to their room. "Thank you for bringing them home."

"Not a problem."

Joel's stomach rumbled. "Down, boy."

"Have you eaten?"

"Not yet."

"I have some leftover pot roast with potatoes and carrots. I'd be happy to warm it up for you."

"You don't need to do that."

"Are you hungry, Joel?"

His grin reminded her of her boys when they wanted something.

"Sit down and I'll warm it up for you. I also have some of the corn bread that I made to go with it."

"You wrestled me down until I had to give up." He held up his hands.

"Does that charm just roll off you without any effort?" she asked as she prepared him a plate.

"No, that's just a hungry cowboy grateful for a good meal. 'Course, don't tell Hank. His cooking has been the mainstay of my diet over the last year and I appreciate him doing the cooking and not me."

The microwave dinged and she pulled the plate out and set it before him. After pouring him a glass of tea, she joined him at the table.

"You were good out there competing, but how that horse missed you, I'll never know. I know the boys were worried." They weren't the only ones. Seeing how close he'd come to getting hurt had taken her breath away.

He paused in devouring the meal and looked up and smiled.

"Cora was worried, too," she hastily added.

He laughed. "She wasn't the only one, was she?"

Looking down at her hands, she whispered, "No."

The humor left his face. "I wasn't hurt."

"But you could've been."

Placing his fork on his plate, he grasped her hand. "Risks are a part of life. Ranching is risky. Driving to a job in the city is risky."

"But the risks in the rodeo are greater than if you worked in an office building in Lubbock."

A slow, heart-stopping smile curved his mouth. "I can imagine lots of jobs I'd like to try. My sis joined the army at eighteen, and I might've liked doing that at her age. Working in the Fort Worth stockyards appealed to me, too, and I might have tried it if my parents had lived. But I know I could never work indoors at an office job. It's not me.

"I'm a cowboy at heart, April. This I know. I wouldn't be happy indoors. I need to see the horizon, feel the wind on my face and breathe the fresh air of the plains. It appeals to and comforts my soul. My dad and granddad shared that feeling."

"Wouldn't you like a steady paycheck for a change?"

He sat back in his chair. "I don't know what that is. My father and grandfather didn't know what that was, either. Price of feed, cattle, whether it rains or there's a drought. I come from a long line of men who've lived with the unknown. That's ranching. And rodeoing. It's who I am."

April couldn't find fault with that. Every rancher in the area lived with that uncertainty. Her father-in-law had always had that insecurity looking over his shoulder.

But his confession confused her. Something wasn't adding up. "So, you're following your dream you had when you were eighteen of going on the rodeo circuit? How does that square with ranching and being outdoors?"

He took the last bite of the pot roast. "Seems strange, doesn't it?"

"Well—"

"Rodeo was quick money to buy my own place, but when that dream turned to ash I concentrated on winning that belt buckle. Haven't you ever had a dream snatched from you, then later had the opportunity to reclaim it?"

"No."

"Really?"

She felt uncomfortable. Had she quit dreaming? The prospect shook her.

"We were talking about rodeo and it being inside you and you not liking working indoors."

She wanted to get the conversation back on him and off her.

He shrugged. "These days, most of the rodeos are indoors, but there are still a few rodeos held outside. Cheyenne Frontier Days is one of them and is like nothing else. Still, the day before performances is nothing like working in an office." He pushed away his plate. "Thank you, April. That was some of the best chow I've eaten in a long time."

She nodded. "I'm used to hungry cowboys."

Reaching for his tea, he took a swallow.

"But you never told me why you wanted to buy your own place and not ranch your family's place."

From the way he hesitated, she wondered if he would answer.

"When you're eighteen, everything seems possible."

His answer touched a raw spot in her heart. She knew.

"I thought I was in love. My girlfriend wanted us to marry straight out of high school and live with her parents." He shook his head. "I couldn't think of anything less appealing than living with my in-laws. She should've just asked me to burn my pride in her parents' backyard."

His story sounded familiar, only she had wanted to live with Ross's parents.

"I couldn't do that, but I could earn enough

money to put a down payment on my own ranch if I rodeoed for a year and made enough. It could stake us. My fiancée didn't like my idea. We fought and broke up.

"I got to thinking maybe she was right and changed my mind and drove out to her parents' ranch to tell her."

He fell silent and April felt her shoulders tighten.

"And?"

"When I pulled into the driveway of her house, my best friend's truck sat in their drive."

April's stomach tightened.

"Unfortunately it was a clear night with a bright quarter moon and I saw my fiancée walking out of the barn picking hay out of her hair. My best friend walked beside her, tucking his shirt into his jeans. When she looked up, I saw the guilt written clearly on her face.

"She ran to my truck to explain. There's no explanation for a betrayal like that. I started the truck and backed out of the driveway."

His story wrapped around her heart. She could identify with his situation. "Did you talk to her?"

"No. What justification could she have given me?"

No answer came to mind.

"I left for the rodeo the next morning. I concentrated on winning that belt buckle. I guess in a way it defined me, gave me a goal and something to concentrate on besides the shame of being dumped. She ran off with my best friend, married and divorced within six months. Of course, the incident on her parents' driveway was the main topic of conversation until my ex-fiancée's divorce. She didn't return home." He shrugged and fell silent.

"What happened after that?"

"I had enough points to go to the finals when the accident happened killing my parents and grandmother. I went home."

Seeing him in the light of his past put his actions in an entirely new light. He was a man who'd given up his dreams for his sister.

"And you left again because of your sister's marriage?"

"How would you feel if your brother lived with you after you married?"

"Both Ross and I were only children and when we married, we came to live here with his parents."

"Oh."

The standoff ended when she grinned. "But I get what you're saying. I loved my in-laws and loved this place. It was my parents who didn't want to stay in one place. Ross loved that. I hated it."

"Well, uh, I wanted to respect Brenda and Caleb's privacy. There are just some things that a brother doesn't need to know. Fortunately, sis thought I might want to try the circuit again. She gave me a good excuse."

April struggled with her grin, but she lost and laughed. Joel joined in.

"Odd, how a tragedy can be turned around. I poured myself into the rodeo, and that broken engagement was just a stepping-stone." He stood, grabbed his plate and placed it in the sink. "Thank you."

Stepping up to the sink next to him, she took the plate. His hand covered hers. She lifted her face to his. "Aren't you going to let go?"

"I was thinking it might cost you a kiss. The one you cheated me out of at the rodeo."

A kiss.

It was just a kiss, but—

His gaze searched hers, probing and asking.

She raised her lips and gently brushed them across Joel's. He didn't let go of the plate but pulled her closer and settled his mouth more firmly over hers. He slipped his arm around her and drew her closer.

Feeling the strength and warmth in his arms eased her heart.

He raised his head and when she opened her eyes, she looked into the fathomless dark brown eyes of this handsome man.

"I'll never think of rinsing off a plate in the same way."

He smiled and turned off the water. "We shouldn't waste the precious water out here."

April stared at the snaps on his Western shirt.

"Are you upset?" His breath disturbed the hair around her ear.

Her head jerked up. "No."

"I was so glad to see you and the kids on the school tour," he confessed.

"The kids missed you, too."

He brushed the back of his hand along her chin. "Were they the only ones?"

She could play coy, but that went against her nature. "No."

"Good. I found myself missing the boys' questions, holding Cora and—their mom." He took her hand and her stomach fluttered. He walked out onto the porch and sat on the swing, pulling her down beside him. "So you married straight out of high school?"

"If you spilled your guts, I should spill mine, too?" she teased.

"I think that's only fair."

He was right. "It's not a very interesting story. When my dad's job brought us out here, he supervised oil platforms, but he'd become an expert at deep-sea oil platforms." She shrugged. "We were always moving for his job.

"Just when I made friends, we had to move. Mom had moving down to an art and always knew how to make friends, but it was harder for me. When we moved here, I knew I'd found my home. This little slice of Texas is where I was meant to be. Somehow this scenery, the very earth, resonated with my soul." She broke off her rambling and glanced at him. "You must think I'm nuts."

"No. I understand exactly what you're saying."

She eyed him, wondering if he was humoring her. But she could detect no insincerity in his eyes.

"Go on."

"I met Ross in high school and fell in love with him." She wondered if it was the ranch and his parents that she really loved instead of Ross. "Ross and I never talked about what we'd do after we married. I thought we'd live here. Ross didn't want to be a rancher. He wanted a job like my father's. I wanted to stay in one place. How opposite was that? We never discussed important stuff, like where we'd live, what Ross would do. I just assumed. So did he."

She'd never confessed her feelings to anyone about Ross. And the things that had tumbled out of her mouth surprised her. "We definitely weren't on the same page."

"I can't cast any stones. I thought I knew my fiancée. I didn't."

"Sounds like we're a pair." Joy bubbled up through her body.

"Do you ever plan to marry again?" Joel asked.

He blinked his eyes as if the question that popped out of his mouth surprised him, too.

"Hadn't planned on it, and definitely won't have more kids."

The phone rang. She hurried inside. "Hello?"

"How are you doing?" Kelly asked.

"Can I call you back?"

"What?" After a moment of silence, Kelly gasped. "Call me later." She hung up.

April rejoined Joel on the bench, wanting their time to continue, but the moment had fled.

"Anything critical?"

"Kelly."

"Ah, girl talk."

"Sometimes friends can help you through the darkest of times. Kelly's that friend."

"I understand." Joel stood. "I guess I need to go."

She regretted their time was over. "Thank you for all you did for the kids. The boys will be talking about this for a long time."

"Now, I should warn you that I invited the boys to share breakfast with the cowboys tomorrow." He shrugged. "I should've checked with you before I said anything."

"I'm glad you warned me."

"Then I'll see you tomorrow morning. I know some of the other cowboys will be willing to help the boys with their twirling."

He studied her and she wanted him to kiss her again.

"'Night." He bent down and brushed a kiss across her lips, then walked to his truck.

She watched him drive out of sight, mooning over their time. He'd kissed her. And he made her laugh. And made her believe that things could be right again. Once back inside, she called Kelly.

"Did I interrupt something?"

With her emotions still whirling, April wasn't going to admit anything. "The boys wanted to help Joel with Spice and we thought it would be a good lesson for them to see how Joel cared for his horse, so the boys stayed and helped him. He brought them home."

"We?"

"Kelly, you really do need to scale back this romance stuff. Joel just brought the boys home, and I fed the man since he doesn't eat before he competes."

"You fed him?"

April wanted to kick herself for making so sloppy a move. "It was leftovers, Kelly, which I fed to a hungry man." Each word made things worse. "What else could I do?"

"You're not hearing any criticism from me. I'm just glad that you took my advice."

April took a deep breath to calm her racing heart. "I enjoyed myself."

"Good."

"But the rodeo leaves Monday morning, and he'll leave with it."

"That's your problem, friend. You're too practical for your own good."

"I know. But the last time I went with only emotions, it didn't work out too well."

"Shame on you, April. You've got three wonderful children, had great in-laws and a family ranch handed down through multiple generations. So what if your husband was— Uh, well, okay, I'm stopping."

April couldn't blame her friend. "I struggle with it, too."

After saying goodbye, April walked out onto the porch and looked into the sky. Kelly's suggestion to enjoy herself had been good, but when those fantasy times came to an end, she and her children would have to face a reality without Joel.

Could she steal one more day before facing that truth? Could she give the kids a few last hours to enjoy this fantasy?

It was only one day. Surely that couldn't hurt. Could it?

Joel nearly ran off the road a couple of times driving back to the auditorium trying to sort out his feelings for April and what had transpired between them. He was getting way too involved with April and her children, but it just felt *so* right, as though he belonged with them.

The boys accepted his direction and eagerly sought it. Cora wanted him to hold her every time he was around her, making him feel ten feet tall.

But it was their mama who tied him up in knots.

He didn't know what to do. When he looked into April's eyes, he saw a different future than he'd imagined, which should've scared him. But it didn't. He could see a family with April, her kids and more babies. Theirs.

He needed to chew on that idea.

Parking the truck beside his horse trailer, Joel just sat in the truck, thinking.

He'd had his life mapped out. Suddenly another road had appeared before him and it didn't lead where he wanted it to go. Slipping out of his truck, he walked to his trailer and leaned against it.

"Congratulations, Joel, on your scores today," Millie called out. Her husband, Mike, walked beside her as they moved to their trailer. "What are you doing out here?"

"Just thinking."

"On what?" Mike asked.

Millie elbowed him.

"What?"

"Men. How are those little cowboys doing? Have they been practicing with their lariats?"

Joel knew Millie had read him perfectly. He opened his mouth to talk but looked at Mike, who appeared clueless and uninterested. Millie mothered all the cowboys and might understand.

Turning to her husband, she said, "Why don't you go get yourself some of that sop cake I made the other day?"

Mike eyed Joel, then his wife, then turned and walked to their trailer.

"So what's up?"

"A lot of confusion, that's what."

"They're a ready-made family, aren't they?"

Joel opened the door to the front compartment of the horse trailer, pulled out the camp chair and set it out for Millie. He parked himself on the trailer stairs.

"I wasn't looking for a ready-made family, Millie. My goal was simply to finish my dream. I'm closer than ever."

"True, and with the scores you got tonight, you're moving in the right direction."

The words were all the right ones, but the tone sounded as though Millie smelled something rotten. Resting his elbows on his knees, Joel shook his head. "Now tell me what you think and not what you think I want to hear."

He raised his head and studied her.

"Are you ready for the truth?"

Pulling his shoulders back, he sat up. "I asked you, Millie."

"But are you ready to hear it?"

"I am."

"God sends us what we need. He also sends us precious gifts. That woman and her babies are a rare gift to treasure for a lifetime. Tell me who won the bareback-riding belt buckle in 1995. And if you know, how does it change your life? What benefit is it to you? To others?"

"But this dream was snatched away once before."

Millie tipped her head and looked at him with one eye. "What price did you pay before? And what price would you pay this time? And is it worth it?" She stood. "You got some serious thinkin' to do, Joel Kaye."

She'd pulled no punches, but that was what he wanted.

"Thanks, Millie. I needed someone who didn't have a dog in this hunt."

She arched her eyebrow. "We'll see." Now he needed to do some serious thinking, and consider Millie's advice and make some decisions.

And prayer wouldn't hurt, either.

Chapter Twelve

April and the children arrived at the venue a little after eight o'clock the next morning. She parked close to Joel's truck and trailer.

The boys had wanted to leave at seven this morning before doing any chores, saying that Joel had invited them for breakfast. She'd made them help with chores before she gave each child a glass of milk to drink. She'd had coffee.

"I don't think Joel was talking about this early."

Wes stopped, turned and held out his hand, striking a pose. "Mom, the cowboys had to feed the stock."

Having her words given back to her made April smile. Apparently, her lessons and seeing Joel work had sunk in.

The boys hurried to the concession area. The voices of the cowboys drifted toward them.

When they rounded the corner, the boys burst into a run.

"Hey, Mr. Joel, we're here," Todd called out.

In the concession area sat several cowboys. Joel was at the table with Millie and Mike, coffee mugs in their hands.

"Look who we have here," Millie said. "Are you boys here to help with the rodeo chores or compete?"

Todd stopped. "No, I'm here to eat breakfast with Mr. Joel." Todd turned to Joel. "Isn't that true?"

"It is."

"I tried feeding them something at home, but they insisted on eating here," April explained. "I would've had more success holding back a dust storm than changing their minds."

Millie patted the place beside her and smiled at Cora. "Would you like to sit between me and Joel?"

Cora nodded and Joel picked her up, settling her between Millie and himself. Millie's eyebrow arched, making April wonder what was going on between Millie and Joel.

Hank appeared quickly with eggs, potatoes and biscuits for the new arrivals.

"I'm glad y'all showed up to begin the day with me." Joel settled back with his coffee and watched the others eat. His gaze rested on April, making her want to smile and laugh. Giddiness bubbled out of her no matter how much she told herself she was way past the age of playing adolescent games.

"Good morning," a tall man called out.

"Reverend Newman," several people greeted.

"Am I in time for breakfast?"

"We just got here," Wes answered. "And Hank brought us breakfast. He'll get you breakfast, too."

"Good to hear," the man answered.

Hank appeared with a coffeepot. "Have you eaten, Charlie?"

"Nope, I wanted to feast on some of your cowboy eggs and biscuits. And drink your coffee. I think you are the envy of all the other rodeos. They credit you with the best coffee going."

Hank cocked his head and his eye squinted. "You're not just pulling my leg, are you?"

"Hank, you're talking to a preacher. I tell the truth."

"Well, I'll be." Hank smiled. "One cowboy special coming up."

"Are you a real minister?" Todd asked.

April's eyes widened. "Son."

Charlie laughed. "I am a real preacher. You should come attend the cowboy church tomorrow morning and hear for yourself."

Both boys turned to her. "Can we, Mom? Please?"

"I've heard about your ministry from Joel. He

says he attends the service when you're at the rodeo. That true?"

"Yes, ma'am, it's true. I can count on Joel to be there."

"Well, I'd like to try it out. But if my pastor questions us as to where we were, I'll have him call you."

Charlie laughed. "I'd be happy to vouch for you."

April listened to the group gathered in the snack area. The good-natured teasing and talking about the day's events warmed her heart.

As Millie and Mike stood to leave, Wes scrambled out from his place at the table.

"Miss Millie," Wes called out.

She stopped and Wes reached into his pocket and pulled out his five dollars.

"Here's the money for my lariat." He held up his money.

Todd hurried to stand beside his brother and reached into his pocket for his money. "I have mine, too."

Millie glanced at April, then back at the boys. Wes's payment was in bills. Todd had a plastic lunch bag filled with coins and bills. He proudly handed his payment to her. "Thank you."

The people who were left in the concession area stopped talking and watched the little drama unfold.

With smiles and their heads held high, Wes and Todd returned to their breakfasts.

"I'm glad you remembered," April told the boys. "I'm proud of you."

"I forgot yesterday, but I wanted to pay Miss Millie," Wes explained.

Joel winked at her. "Nice job."

His encouragement made her proud that her boys had learned the lessons she'd been trying to teach them.

As the morning wore on, her kids followed Joel like little ducks following their mother. He introduced them to everyone in the rodeo who hadn't already met the kids.

About ten-thirty, as the boys took another lesson in throwing a lariat, Cora lay down on a bale of hay and fell asleep.

Joel nodded to the little girl. "Let me put her in my trailer, which I think she'll find more comfortable than that prickly bale of hay." He didn't wait for April to okay it, but scooped up Cora and walked to his trailer. He nodded toward the door. "Want to open that for me?"

April complied and Joel laid Cora on his bed. The clean compartment didn't surprise April. Cora clutched her horsey in her arms as she curled into a ball.

"I'm worried if she wakes up in a strange place, she'll panic."

"No problem." Joel pushed the door open until it clicked into place. "This way when she wakes, she can see outside. If you put your chair in her line of sight, there won't be a problem."

The man seemed to have an answer for everything. She didn't have to worry. It was such an unusual experience for April that she didn't know how to act.

"While Cora's napping, I'll keep the boys busy."

His offer made her smile. "Thank you."

The boys quickly disappeared, leaving April in a unique situation with nothing to do.

"Those boys of yours are a dynamic duo," Millie said, walking toward April.

"I didn't know they wanted to be cowboys so bad."

Millie nodded toward a chair by the next trailer. "Mind if I sit with you?"

"Please do."

Millie pulled the chair close and settled in it, saying nothing.

"I want to thank you for giving Cora the stuffed horse. That horse is with her at all times."

"My granddaughters like it, and your little one had that same look in her eye that my granddaughters had."

"Where do they live?" April asked.

"Santa Fe. My son there works for the city,

bringing in more visitors and business. I only get to see them when the rodeo is in New Mexico."

"So you raised a son who wasn't a cowboy?"

It looked as if April had pinched the older woman. "No, he and his brother are cowboys, raised in the culture. Our daughter does barrel racing. We lived in a small city south of Santa Fe. My husband owned an auto shop and worked on all the cowboys' trucks and rodeo vehicles. One day a vendor came to the shop to have his truck worked on. He wanted to retire. Mike bought his business, and we sold the auto shop." She shrugged. "It's been fun."

April didn't understand the woman's attitude. "Doesn't the constant moving wear on you?"

"No. We stayed in the same place to raise our kids, so they were all grown when we changed our lives. Doing this job seemed like an adventure. During the summer, our granddaughters travel with us and have the time of their lives."

April couldn't wrap her mind around it.

"I take it you don't want to travel."

"It's the last thing on my mind."

"It takes a certain kind of person. But I think if I'd done this when my boys were young, it would've been harder with their schooling and them having friends. I know Joel had a time of adjustment when he first came on the circuit. He isn't like the young'uns who want to party and brag."

"You mean he isn't serious about winning that belt buckle?" Maybe there was hope.

"No, that isn't what I said. That man's dead serious about his competition. The championship belt is important to all these cowboys, but they play on the way. Joel is single-minded. I know he was on the circuit when he was young. This time, it's almost like he knows this is his last chance and he's not going to miss it."

"I see."

Millie looked in the trailer. "I'm glad your little one likes that horse I gave her."

"She hasn't let it out of her sight. At bath time, the horse has to watch from the counter. If Cora had her way, he would've taken a bath with her."

"Good."

"And the boys have practiced with their lariats every moment they can. We've gone to trying to rope each other."

Millie laughed. "You've got boys. What else can you expect?"

Seeing her boys through Millie's eyes made her smile. It also made her realize how they'd come to life after Joel showed up at their ranch. "Good point."

Joel had brought them all a renewal.

Millie continued to chat, but April's mind concentrated on how Joel had changed them all for the better.

* * *

The morning passed in a whirlwind of activity. Joel made sure the boys talked to the cowboys who specialized in various events, telling them what was required. They also shared how they'd gotten into rodeo. Amazingly enough, every man encouraged the boys to finish school and try college, much to April's obvious surprise, judging by her face. She and Cora joined the groups after Cora finished a short nap.

"Several colleges offer rodeo scholarships. And those colleges also offer courses in animal husbandry, crop rotation and farm and ranch management," Ty Newsome said. "That's what I'm going for."

Joel stepped behind April. Her fragrance—vanilla—made him lose track of what he wanted to say.

Glancing over her shoulder, she frowned.

"Makes you see the guys in a different light, doesn't it?" he whispered. He nodded toward the cowboys gathered around her boys.

"Yes, but if you're going to be on the circuit, you have to travel, and not stay in one place and develop roots."

"True."

"And what of their families and loved ones who are waiting back home?"

"What about the four years an average student is away from home to get a college degree?" he replied.

She frowned and turned back to listen to Ty talk to the boys.

Those young minds didn't run out of questions.

After about twenty minutes, Cora tugged on April's jeans. "Go see horsey lady."

"Apparently Cora's not interested in the finer points of bull riding. We'll be with Millie."

Joel watched her and Cora make their way to the souvenir stand. He could understand her objection to the traveling, moving one place to another. It had taken him some getting used to, but couldn't she see the short-term discomfort for a long-term goal?

Had she been that burned by her husband being away? Could she accept a man who traveled?

After the last cowboy finished, the boys and Joel walked to the holding pen housing the calves for the calf scramble.

"I did this event last year," Wes informed him.

An idea formed in Joel's head. "Todd, have you done the calf scramble?"

"No, but Opa said I could probably do it this year."

"Why don't you stay here with Ty? I'll be back in a moment."

Joel went in search of April and found her talking to Kelly at the souvenir stand.

"So how's your husband feeling about having to buy all new baby things since you got rid of everything after your youngest outgrew them?" April asked.

Joel paused. He didn't want to barge into the conversation.

"He's a little shell-shocked still, but the things we have to get cost less than the new tractor he wants, so he's okay with it. Really, he's getting excited."

Joel cleared his throat.

"I guess you overheard," Kelly said.

"I did. Congratulations."

"Thank you." Kelly's eyes widened, then she rushed off to the ladies' room.

"Is she all right?" Joel asked.

April shook her head. "Looks like she has a case of morning sickness."

"It's eleven." Joel frowned.

"Babies don't tell time, as you should well know, dealing with foals and calves, puppies and kittens."

"You're right. I wasn't thinking." He stepped closer and lowered his voice. He didn't want to cause a scene if April refused to allow the boys to participate. "Would you object if your kids entered the calf scramble?"

"Both boys?"

"According to Todd, their grandfather thought he would be able to do it this year."

"Do you think he could do it?"

"Yes. I don't know if either boy would catch the calf, but they'd have fun trying."

"They aren't registered."

"I can take care of that," he reassured her.

"But—"

"Let your boys try it and have some fun," Millie said.

Both Joel and April turned to Millie.

"You're both terrible at whispering." She grinned. "And my hearing is exceptional."

"I'm being ganged up on here," April complained. After a moment, she nodded.

Joel brushed a kiss across her cheek. "Your boys are up next." He took two steps and stopped. "They'll have helmets."

As he rushed back, he saw Millie grin and say something to April, which made her smile.

What was going on there?

The balance of the day seemed like a wonderful dream. Neither boy won the calf scramble, but their laughter and joy made them both winners.

Joel added points to his two event totals, and the boys yelled so much for Joel that they lost their voices and only could whisper by the end of the evening.

As they left the auditorium, April carried a sleepy Cora, while Joel carried a tuckered-out Todd. All her children's energy levels registered empty.

"Can I go in Joel's truck?" Wes asked.

April stopped and turned to Joel. He didn't offer an opinion or objection as much as he wanted to. He wanted to know if she'd welcome him after the closeness they'd experienced last night and their day together.

"Joel would have to drive out to the ranch, and he's tired, too, son."

"I don't mind." He wanted to spend more time with the kids.

Get real. Two of the three children are asleep. You want the time with their mother.

"Okay."

Wes smiled.

After all the kids were strapped in the car seats, April headed home, with Joel's truck following close behind.

Glancing over at Wes in the passenger seat, Joel asked, "Did you have a good time today?"

"I did. It was the best day ever. I'll be able to tell the other guys at school about the cowboys, how they ride and how some are going to college."

"Did you ever consider college?"

"No. Did you go?"

"No, I didn't, and every day, I regret it. But

I've taken courses from the state university south of my family's ranch. Learning is never wasted. It gives me ideas on how to deal with the animals on the ranch and how to manage money."

Wes nodded. He stared down at his folded hands.

Joel waited for the boy to speak his piece. He had something on his mind, and Joel needed to give the boy the time and space to lasso the words.

"Could you stay with us after the rodeo leaves?" Wes hurriedly asked, never looking up. "If you like Mom, maybe you could marry her and live here with us."

The words ambushed him. Who would've thought Wes a matchmaker in jeans and boots?

"I know Todd and Cora want you to stay, too. Cora always wants you to hold her," Wes added for good measure.

"I'm honored by your request."

Wes lifted his head, hope and excitement in his eyes.

"But when two people marry, it's because they love each other and want to spend their lives together."

"I thought you liked Mom. I saw you kiss her."

Clearly, things were going downhill and they'd been caught. "Marriage is a serious step, not something to be rushed into."

"Isn't it serious when you kiss someone?"

"Yes." He wanted to explain more, but Wes plunged on.

"My oma—that's what we called Grandma— said her mother came to Lubbock to marry her father without knowing him. And she didn't kiss him, either."

Wes had neatly trapped him. "It does happen, but when did your great-grandmother come out here?"

"I don't know."

"A lot of things have changed in the last hundred years. Your great-grandmother may have come on a train, or stagecoach, or by wagon. There were no cars or phones or computers with email."

"Oh."

"But I know it took courage for your great-grandmother to do what she did."

"So the answer's no."

Joel's heart jerked at the boy's despondent remark.

"Well, I'd have to ask your mom, and she'd have to say yes."

He perked up. "So why don't you ask her?"

Good question. Joel had to admit the notion had floated around his brain, and once Wes had verbalized the words, they seemed to take hold of his heart.

He smiled at Wes. "We'll see."

Chapter Thirteen

Once home, April tried to interest the children in dinner. None wanted to eat, and all fell into bed.

"I guess that's what happens when you eat continuously all day long. I hope they don't wake up with tummy aches." She shook her head and smiled. "I'm sure they'll tell me it was worth it."

"I remember the time my folks took me to the rodeo in Fort Worth. I think I was eleven at the time. I ate myself sick, despite my mom's warnings, but I learned my lesson and didn't do it again."

"Let's see how they react." She knew she wouldn't forget this day, either. "Now that the kids are in bed, I've got animals that need tending." She started out to the barn and Joel followed her.

"You don't have to help."

"I know."

She stopped and stared at him. His obligation was over, so why help? Had Ross so warped her view of young men that she assumed there was a motive behind everything Joel did? There had been for Ross.

"What?" He cupped her cheek and his gaze searched hers. "Tell me."

"It's nothing. Usually I don't have an adult helping me do these chores. Well, not since Vernon died."

"I'm here and it's the right thing to do. The Christian thing."

The man managed to knock down every excuse, every reason she could come up with to run the opposite direction from him. He didn't run from work, he helped others and her children adored him. No question was too stupid, no excuse why it couldn't get done.

As they worked together on the chores, she said, "I hope Wes wasn't too much trouble. I know you have to be dead tired, and driving out here was out of your way."

"I didn't mind."

She knew there was more to that sentence, but she couldn't put her finger on it.

When they walked into the kitchen, April felt tongue-tied and self-conscious. Joel took off his hat and hung it on the hook by the back door. As she stared at his hat, it seemed way too intimate, as if he were the man of the house.

"Have you eaten?"

He flushed. "No. I would've gotten something from Hank, but things got crazy toward the end of the night."

"All I have to offer is bologna sandwiches, since someone ate the rest of the roast last night."

"It was a good roast. But a sandwich sounds great." He settled at the kitchen table.

Being alone with Joel in the kitchen at the end of the day felt too homey. "Todd enjoyed himself so much that he wasn't the least bit embarrassed about falling asleep."

"Well, cowboys, even little shavers like him, have their pride. But he had fun."

"Seeing all the kids enjoying themselves was—" She swallowed. "I didn't realize how much of a downer I'd become." She choked back her tears.

Suddenly Joel's strength and warmth were at her back.

"Don't be so hard on yourself. You've had a lot on your plate."

She leaned back against him, soaking up his strength. His arms slid around her waist. He rested his chin on the top of her head. "So far, I haven't been doing too well."

"You've got great kids."

She nodded and concentrated on making the sandwiches. "Sorry I don't have something more, uh—adult. I do have peanut butter and jelly. But with the bologna I've got lettuce, tomatoes, pickles and sweet peppers if you want."

"Hey, I've been known to pack my own peanut-butter-and-grape-jelly sandwiches when Gramps and I were out working the ranch."

"PBJ? At your age, I'm impressed."

"Hey, there's nothing better than PBJ. It's saved my bacon at the end of a long day more than once. Gramps even loved them."

She piled the plates with sandwiches and chips and placed them on the table. "Coffee?"

"Anytime, anywhere."

She poured only one cup of coffee and a glass of water and placed them on the table.

"Water?"

"If I drink coffee late, I don't sleep well." She didn't need to add that phenomenon had only occurred since he showed up at the ranch.

After a quick prayer, they started eating.

April stood and opened one of the cabinet doors, reached to the back, pulled out a Twinkie and set it before him.

"Ah, you know how to win a man's heart."

His statement hung in the air.

"Those are the boys' favorite. I hide them and get them out as a reward."

"Is this a reward for me?"

"Yes." April blushed at the implication. She hadn't meant to suggest that, but maybe subconsciously she had. "You deserve this for all your help. And you've shown us how to have fun."

He picked up the Twinkie and grinned. "I'd forgotten how much I loved these. When I found it in the lunch you packed for me, it was a treat." He put the treat down and tore into his sandwich. "My mom used these as rewards, too, but both my father and grandfather sneaked them all the time. When she wanted to give one to me or my sister, she'd find them all gone. So she started buying two boxes and hid one in her laundry room. She knew that neither my dad nor Gramps would darken the door of the laundry room."

A sense of contentment settled over her as she watched Joel wolf down the food she'd made him. She wouldn't tell him about the crazy calls she'd gotten from the school and the outlandish assumptions her neighbors and friends were making.

"Folks at the rodeo mention your boys, impressed with their eagerness. Most of the guys told me how old they were when they joined the rodeo and what they were doing when they were Wes's and Todd's ages. A lot of reminiscing and funny stories surfaced that made us laugh. Those stories let your sons know they're regular boys. It encouraged them."

His words were balm to her battered soul. Maybe she'd done something right, supported by her in-laws.

Once Joel finished the last of his sandwich, he opened the Twinkie.

The production he made of eating the treat made her laugh. "You weren't kidding, were you?"

"There are some things you never outgrow."

She fell silent, thinking about what Millie had told her.

"I saw you and Millie talking."

"She told me about how Mike and she went on the road. She also talked about you."

He stilled. "Oh?"

"She said you were serious about winning that belt buckle. And that you weren't like the younger cowboys. Is that buckle that important to you?"

He stood and reached down for her hand and pulled her outside to the porch swing. They settled by each other and he slipped his arm around her shoulders. "A couple of years ago my church put together a charity rodeo to help the ranchers who were suffering through the drought. As I worked on it, something inside me woke up. I didn't realize it at the time, but when my sister started questioning me about my whistling, I stopped and thought about it. I used to whistle a lot as a teen. When I came home after the accident, I don't remember whistling until we started organizing the rodeo. Sis keyed in on that. I don't think I would've gone back on the circuit without her encouragement, but as I thought about it, I knew I had to try to fulfill that promise."

April held her breath.

"But meeting a certain widow and her children has put other ideas in my head."

She could breathe again.

"I've been thinking about life after this rodeo season. I won't make another year of traveling and doing a rodeo every week, three or four competitions at each stop. My aches have aches."

"So, have you come to any conclusion on what you might do?"

He hugged her. "Well, it depends on how a certain lady feels."

"About what?"

"About a certain older cowboy who'd like to try ranching again."

Her mouth went dry. "Where would that cowboy like to ranch?"

He looked around. "I don't know. He hasn't made up his mind, but he's been looking."

"Well, he might want to try out here in the Panhandle, because a certain lady rancher will not move and leave her children's inheritance. That ranch has been in their family for five generations. And she will not have any more kids."

He paused. "Sounds reasonable when your roots are that deep in the soil, as if the very ground becomes part of your soul. I don't think that cowboy has thought it through. He's just flying by the seat of his pants and would have to think on it."

He opened his mouth to say something more, then snapped it shut. After a moment, he said, "I need to go and let you get some rest. Thanks for the bologna sandwich and Twinkie." He pulled her to her feet and brushed a kiss across her lips. "See you tomorrow?"

Later that night, April lay in bed wide-awake. Her body complained, exhausted from the day's activity, but her mind didn't heed the message.

What had just happened? She'd thought he'd put out that story about the old cowboy as a dry run for a marriage proposal, then poof, he'd up and said goodbye. What had spooked him? Was it her saying she wouldn't have any more kids?

He'd thrown her a major curve. She didn't understand.

Okay, she'd fantasized about what it would be like to have Joel here all the time, helping her with the ranch and being there for the children. But the sticking point was Joel traveling, following the rodeo. They hadn't talked about it. Instead he'd asked if she'd love an old cowboy. That she could do without any problems. She was no spring chicken herself. But from their talks, he sounded as though he wanted to finish pursuing that prize belt buckle this year. Could she live with that?

Sitting up in bed, she put her pillow behind her back. "Can I do that?" she whispered. Could she buy him finishing this year?

She didn't know. And if he finished this year on the circuit, would he be satisfied once he won the belt buckle?

And if he didn't win, would he want to try again next year? He said he didn't, but how invested was he in this dream? What would it take for him to be satisfied? She'd lived through that nightmare before, and she didn't want to go for round two. And there was more than her to consider.

With each question, a little more of her joy and excitement drained out.

She'd made some stupid mistakes when she'd been eighteen, jumping into marriage without knowing what she was getting into. She would *not* make that mistake again.

Satisfied with her decision, she drifted off to sleep. The last thing she thought about was Joel walking out to the barn with her, willing to help with chores.

What a romantic she was.

Joel woke with a start. He heard the boom of lightning. He opened the door to the trailer, but there was no rain. In the distance, Joel saw the sky blink with strikes of lightning. Of course he knew how wicked lightning could be, since his family's ranch had once taken a direct hit, frying every bit of electronic equipment in the house including the fifty-inch flat-screen TV Gramps and he had mounted on the living room wall.

He slipped on his short boots and checked Spice, who was still housed in the auditorium building. He ran into Jack.

"Are you here to check on your horse?" Jack asked. He wore just a T-shirt, jeans and running shoes.

"Yeah. Spice is normally calm if she's inside." He glanced at the corral. The horses moved about the enclosure, listening, agitated.

"Let's hope the storm ends quickly and doesn't come our way."

"I'll stay here and keep watch on the horses," Joel offered. "You can go back to bed."

"Naw, I won't go to sleep until things settle down. Besides, if the horses get spooked, you'll need more than one man, unless you've turned into one of those superheroes that are so popular. We could call you Cowboy Man."

"Boy, waking you isn't a pretty thing, is it?"

Jack laughed. "That's what my wife always says."

They found two folding chairs and placed them against the wall.

Conflicting thoughts and emotions twisted through Joel, much like the twisters that plague Texas in the spring. Earlier this evening when

Wes had asked him to stay, the notion had shot straight to his heart, focusing all those feelings Joel had been dancing around. Where that old-cowboy story had come from, he had no idea. But once the words were out of his mouth, he'd gotten cold feet. He wanted to think about it.

"Your thoughts are so loud I couldn't sleep if I wanted to," Jack said, stopping Joel's internal debate.

"What?"

"Something's got you hopped up and concerned."

"Were you married when you won your belt buckle for bull riding?"

"No, but I was engaged. She wanted me to stop."

"But it was after you won, right?"

"We had a deal. I did rodeo the season after we married, but it was hard on her, and when she got pregnant, well, I couldn't travel worried about her and the baby."

"So how'd you get back into rodeo?" Joel rubbed his chin.

"I never let my contacts lag and ten years ago, Steve Carter needed someone to step into the role of manager. Since I wasn't going to do events and my company was downsizing, the job appeared at the right time and I had no objections from the wife. Why? Are you thinking of taking the plunge?"

"Could be." But before he could explain further, thunder rattled the building. The horses panicked. Soaked cowboys came running, ropes in hand, in case they needed to catch some of the more agitated horses.

The downpour lasted only ten minutes. Once the excitement died down, everyone went to bed.

Joel walked to his trailer. After shucking off his boots, he stretched out on the bed.

He loved April, plain and simple. And he loved her family, which meant he would be staying in the Panhandle. That wasn't a problem. He'd saved up enough money to buy his own place, but he could put that money in the Circle L, updating some of the equipment.

It felt right. He could imagine the kids growing up and adding more children of their own. Her saying she wouldn't have any more babies probably was her just saying she didn't want to try again. Being married, she might want another one.

Not competing next year wasn't a problem, since he hadn't planned on it anyway. But if he didn't finish this season, would he regret it?

He wrestled with the problem the rest of the night.

Chapter Fourteen

"Mom, Mom, get up." A small hand shook her arm.

April opened one eye to be greeted by Todd's smiling face. It took several moments for her brain to kick into gear, since she hadn't fallen asleep until after three.

"It's time to get up. We're going to cowboy church, and we don't want to be late."

She glanced at the clock. Five-thirty. Todd never got up at this time. He raced off, leaving her to get her bearings. She tossed and turned, going over everything Joel had said last night. Their conversation had left her scratching her head. What had he been trying to say?

Two weeks ago, she'd felt alone, deserted and wondering how things would work out. The prayer she'd uttered the morning Joel showed up ran through her mind. God had sent help. Not in the way she expected it, but He'd sent help.

Now she had her fields planted and the fences around the ranch secured so she wouldn't lose any of her cattle, and those chores she'd hadn't gotten to since her father-in-law died had been taken care of. Everything was right, but her heart wanted more.

She wanted Joel to stay. Be a husband and a father.

But as joy and confusion bubbled up, another stark reality appeared. Maybe, just maybe, she'd never really loved Ross at all. Maybe she'd loved the ranch, his family and having a home she didn't have to leave every eighteen months instead of loving the man himself. Was that the reason he'd hired on as an oil-field worker—because she hadn't loved him enough? Or maybe he'd regretted marrying her and just walked away.

Neither answer appealed to her.

Todd appeared again at her bedroom door, his superhero T-shirt wet with milk. "Uh, I kinda made a mess."

April grabbed her robe, slipped it over her supermom sleep shirt and followed her son into the kitchen, ready to mop up milk.

Wes walked into the main bathroom, where April worked on putting Cora's hair into pigtails. Cora sat on the vanity counter.

"You ready, son?"

"I am."

Wes had his I'm-worried-about-something expression on.

April didn't push.

"Mom, I want Joel to stay here with us."

April dropped the ribbon she was tying in Cora's hair. "Really?"

"I asked him to stay last night when he drove me home, but he said he couldn't because we'd have to make sure it was okay with you." His brows furrowed and he fixed her with his dark eyes.

She picked up the ribbon, scrambling for an answer. "Well, he was right."

"So why aren't you okay with marrying Mr. Joel?"

She was, but he'd have to propose first. "Have you decided to take up matchmaking as a career? The Cowboy Matchmaker?"

"Huh? A matchmaker? What's that?"

"A long time ago, there were women you would go to who would match a man and woman so they could get married."

"Like the commercials on TV?"

"What commercials?" Todd asked, coming into the bathroom, looking around.

"TV commercials about dating," Wes explained.

"Ick."

Ignoring her younger son's comment, she answered, "Yes, that's how it worked. So are you taking on that role?"

"No, I just want Mr. Joel to stay 'cause he makes us all laugh. And he makes you laugh and smile. It's been a long time since you did that, Mom."

"That's true," Todd added. "I forgot that you could laugh."

The boys' words, so simple and honest, stabbed her in the heart. Leaning over, she brushed a kiss across Wes's cheek, then Todd's. "Thank you, boys."

"For what?"

"For telling me I should laugh."

At their frowns, she laughed.

"So do you want Mr. Joel to stay?" Wes pressed.

"He'd have to ask."

Wes nodded at her answer. "Okay."

Joel helped set up the platform for Charlie to preach from. Section D in the auditorium was where the people for cowboy church would sit to see Charlie. Joel also found a stool for the guitarist to use as he led the crowd in worship.

Buck walked onto the dirt floor, holding his guitar.

"Is this good for you?" Joel asked.

"It is." Buck moved to the stool, settled on it and played a few chords.

Joel checked that everything was in place, then walked off the auditorium floor and listened as Buck practiced a worship chorus. Leaning back against the wall of the entrance walkway, Joel listened to the song, trying to ignore the excitement and joy bouncing around inside him at seeing April and her crew.

When he woke this morning, he'd known what he would do. Before the end of the day, he'd propose, and he felt sure she'd say yes. Until he laid eyes on April again and confirmed her feelings for himself, his heart wouldn't believe this dream could come true.

"O how he loves me." The words drifted out of the auditorium.

Okay, Lord, I don't know what to do here. Joel closed his eyes. Details needed to be worked out. And lots of issues had to be resolved between April and him, but—

"What are you doing out here?" Ty asked.

"Waiting for people to get here."

Grinning, Ty said, "I can guess who."

"Kinda obvious."

"Only if you have eyes in your head."

Joel frowned.

"Is there something more we should know about you and April?"

"What are you talking about?" Joel tried to keep his expression neutral.

"Mr. Joel," Wes called out, waving as he ran toward Joel.

Ty slapped Joel on the shoulder. "You don't need to answer." He walked into the auditorium.

Joel turned and watched as the Landers family came toward him. His stomach jumped and a smile spread across his face. He felt tongue-tied and self-conscious. "Good morning, Wes, Todd and Cora." Cora let go of her mother's hand and ran toward him.

He scooped the girl up and realized how he treasured the greeting the children gave him, like a warm homecoming. Turning, he shared a secret smile with April. Her eyes twinkled, making him want to lean over and plant a kiss on her lips in front of the kids and the other cowboys and people walking around the halls. He had the confirmation he wanted. She shared his feelings. He hadn't imagined it.

"The children were eager to come see you and participate in the cowboy church."

"Just the kids?"

"No." Her voice dropped low.

"I hear music," Todd commented. "C'mon."

They followed the youngsters into the seating area inside the auditorium. The boys greeted the other people as they wandered up and down the steps.

The family quickly settled into a section in front of the preaching platform.

Wes tugged on Joel's sleeve. "I need to talk to you."

"Okay."

Wes shook his head. "Now and in private."

"We'll be back in a moment."

The instant they were outside the auditorium, Wes stopped and motioned Joel to lean down.

"Mom would say yes if you asked her to marry you."

Joel jerked upright.

"I told Mom about our conversation and what you said."

"And what did she say?"

"She smiled and laughed. I think she'd say yes, but you'd have to ask."

Joel wanted to laugh himself. "Thanks for telling me."

"So are you going to ask?"

"I think I will, but you have to keep the secret until I can talk to your mom."

Wes beamed. "I can do that."

They walked back into the auditorium, and Wes scampered to his seat. Joel sat by April.

Leaning close, April whispered, "What was that about?"

"Just man-to-man talk."

She looked straight into his eyes. The urge to escape with her and find a private spot and propose nearly overwhelmed him.

Millie and her husband walking up the stairs and sitting beside him in the row ended that plan.

"Stop that," Millie whispered.

"What?" Joel tried to look innocent.

"We're going to have a service and you're ogling a girl, then fibbing about it."

He'd been caught.

Cora smiled at Millie and showed her the horsey.

"So you still like your horse?"

Nodding, Cora hugged the stuffed animal.

The beginning chords of the worship chorus came over the speaker, and the audience stood and joined in with the song.

Leaning close, Millie added, "While Charlie is here, you should just book him for the wedding."

Joel jerked away. "What?"

"You two are lit up like neon lights."

"Things aren't official."

"So, you can take care of that. If you don't want to give anything away, I suggest that you shouldn't look at April all moon-eyed." She grinned, turned and joined in with the chorus.

Joel focused on the podium, trying to be cool.

It wasn't working. He could feel Millie grinning beside him as they finished the worship service.

Suddenly the sermon ended and everyone stood and sang the final song. Joel remembered nothing of the sermon. Had Charlie preached?

Filing out of the auditorium, Joel grabbed Millie. "Could you watch the kids for a moment?"

Millie gave him a knowing look.

"I'm going to take your advice."

"About time."

Joel grabbed April's hand. "Millie's going to take the kids to the snack area."

"Why?"

Joel glanced at Wes and winked. "Mom, I'll hold Cora's hand."

Without further discussion, Joel pulled April to the front door of the building, where it was quiet.

"What are you doing?" she asked.

"Trying to find us a quiet spot."

April blushed.

He found a bench just inside the front doors and they sat. Joel swallowed. "Little did I know when I drove up your drive nearly two weeks ago, I would find a wonderful family and a beautiful woman who knocked me flatter than any bull I've tried to ride, but I did.

"One look in your eyes and I knew. Deep in my heart I knew here was the one. I couldn't shake it off.

"And your children just took me by storm. I didn't have a chance." He shook his head. "I'm going to be such an easy mark for Cora."

"She knows how to work her wiles already.

I'm sure she's going to be a handful when she's grown." April smiled.

"And Wes and Todd are sharp boys. I nearly fell off the loading dock when they wanted to hire me to help you with the planting."

"I didn't believe you until the boys confirmed your story. I would've loved to have seen that scene play out."

They exchanged chuckles.

He grabbed her hand. "I love you, April. Love you and your children. Will you marry me?"

Her gaze searched his face, looking for the truth of his words.

His lips brushed over hers, reassuring her. "Yes."

He leaned his forehead against hers. "I am blessed."

Tears filled her eyes. "I had my back up against the wall and didn't know how I'd make it. I'd just said amen when you drove up. You weren't what I was expecting." Her fingers danced over his face, as if she was blind. "But God certainly knows what He's doing."

"Mom," Todd called out. He ran up to them and noted the tears in his mother's eyes. "Are you okay?" His gaze narrowed as he turned to Joel.

"She's okay," Joel reassured the boy.

"Why's she crying?"

"Because I'm happy," April answered.

"Huh?"

Joel laughed. "It's a girl thing."

Todd's brow remained crinkled.

Joel leaned forward and whispered, "Your mom and I are getting married."

Todd let loose with a whoop that rang through the hall, and he raced back to the concession area yelling, "They're getting married!"

When they arrived back at the picnic tables, everyone broke into applause. Wes gave Joel a thumbs-up. Cora ran to Joel. He scooped her up and she wrapped her arms around his neck.

Congratulations were called out. Chaos erupted with the cowboys slapping Joel on the back and shaking April's hand. The boys bounced around.

"So when's this going to happen?" Millie asked.

"Joel and I haven't discussed particulars yet."

April's answer brought a smile to Millie's face.

"I never would've guessed," Mike said, shaking his head.

"Men are so obtuse," Millie mumbled.

"What's *obtuse*?" Todd asked, looking at Millie.

"It means a man can instantly tell if you scratched his truck, but he can't see two people in love right in front of his face," Millie answered.

"We need to celebrate," Hank announced. "I'd planned to feed everyone to use up what I had left before we move to our next stop in Amarillo, but now we have extra reason to celebrate."

"I have a sop cake I made for Mike yesterday," Millie added. "We can use that for an engagement cake if you don't mind a couple of pieces missing." Millie looked at her husband. Mike shrugged, bringing a round of laughter to the crowd.

Joel kept glancing at April, wondering at her reaction. After Millie went to retrieve the cake, Joel fought his way to April's side.

"Are you okay announcing it now?"

"I guess the goofy expressions on our faces would've tipped everyone off."

"Could be, but I just couldn't keep it a secret. Apparently neither could Todd."

The soft, sweet smile she gave him nearly brought him to his knees.

"Did you know that Wes made a pitch for you this morning while I was putting Cora's hair in pigtails?"

"Oh?"

"Wes liked how you made me smile. And laugh."

The words wrapped around his heart. "I'm glad to know Wes is in my corner."

Joel slipped his arm around her waist and whispered, "I think your boys are okay with us marrying if their happy dance is any indication. And we don't have to worry about Cora, either."

That was the last time he talked to April for the next hour. Hank, Ty, Buck and Millie peppered him with questions.

"Are you going to quit right away, Joel, and give away your chance for a belt buckle?" Ty asked.

His question reverberated through the snack area, silencing all conversation.

"April and I haven't discussed it yet," Joel explained. "But—"

Hank turned to April. "He's close, April. You might want to wait. The prize money is very nice and goes a long way in helping a rancher."

April's mouth tightened.

"I think April and I need to work this out privately and not in front of an audience. And you don't have voting power."

Laughter rippled in response.

"So you two planning on adding more children to the kids you have already?" Millie asked, bringing all conversation to a halt once more.

"Of course," Joel answered quickly. "I can't think of anything I'd like more."

When he glanced at April, she was as white as a sheet.

Something was wrong. Deadly wrong.

But what?

April tried to respond to the questions folks asked her, but her world suddenly went up in flames.

Joel wanted children. His own.

She'd told him she wouldn't have any more children, so why would he say he wanted kids?

Had he forgotten? Or did he think she just didn't want more kids because she felt she'd had enough already? Did he think she had an option?

Joel caught her eye. He shrugged as if to say he was sorry his friends asked such personal questions.

And there were her kids' reactions. They wanted Joel and her to marry and expected him to stay.

She couldn't stay here and pretend everything was fine. Too much had gone wrong that she needed to sort out, and she needed to get away before she made a scene.

Cora began to droop, giving her the perfect excuse. "I think we need to leave." April pointed to Cora.

Joel pushed the hair off of Cora's face. "She could sleep in the trailer again."

"No, she needs to go home." Her sharp tone made him pause.

"The boys could stay here—"

"They need to come home with me, too."

Joel stared at her, but she needed time and space.

Wes and Todd looked from their mom to Joel, but they didn't object.

"Okay."

Before she could grab Cora from the picnic bench, Joel scooped her up. He didn't look back at her but slowly walked toward the parking lot. Wes and Todd trailed after him.

April found her purse and snatched it from the floor.

Millie laid a hand on April's arm. "The guys meant no harm. Don't let them bother you."

Her throat tightened. "It wasn't the guys."

"Then what?"

"There are some issues that Joel and I need to talk about that we didn't discuss before." April closed her eyes and took a deep breath. "I need to go home and think about them."

"I understand, but know Joel is a find that lots of women would like to catch. I wouldn't turn my back on him."

April nodded, trying not to break down in tears and frighten her children.

Joel stood by her truck. He had a puzzled look on his face. Wes and Todd stood beside him, subdued. April clicked the automatic door locks, opening the truck. Joel strapped Cora in her seat while April helped Todd.

When she walked to the driver's door, Joel caught her arm.

"What's wrong?" he whispered. "I hope you're not upset Todd told everyone."

Refusing to look at him, she said, "No, I'm not upset with that." Slipping by him, she got into the driver's seat.

"I'll be by later."

Still not meeting his gaze, she nodded, started the truck and drove off.

The fairy tale had lasted less than a few hours. But at least she'd had a moment.

Joel stood in the parking lot watching April speed away.

"I don't know what happened there," Jack said. "I hope the cowboys didn't upset her."

Rubbing the back of his neck, Joel was clueless. "I honestly don't know, but something went wrong."

"I'd give her some time before you try to talk to her." Jack shook his head. "Women are curious creatures that not a cowboy in this place knows how to deal with. Bulls, horses, cows, calves, we've got it nailed, but women are beyond understanding. Too bad they don't come with instruction manuals like I have on my truck and tractor."

Truer words were never spoken.

The cowboys packed up what they could that afternoon so Monday morning they could load the livestock and head on out to Amarillo.

Joel listened for his cell to ring all afternoon, but so far, nothing. He searched his brain as to what was said that had upset April. The other cowboys had been teasing them about marriage and kids.

When Millie asked him if they'd have another

child, he'd automatically said yes. From April's reaction, something was wrong, but what?

"Haven't heard from April?" Millie asked, stopping by his trailer.

"No. Do you have any clue what upset her?" At this point he was desperate.

Tapping her lips with her finger, Millie thought. "Can't say as if I could tell you, but a face-to-face with the woman is the best way for you to deal with things. You can see her reactions to what you're saying to know if you're right or wrong. Go out there."

He stood and brushed a kiss across her cheek. "Thanks for the good advice."

"Hope you get things straightened out with April."

"Thanks."

As he drove out to the ranch, he prayed for the understanding he needed to fix the problem and the grace to do it.

When he drove up to the ranch, he saw all three kids sitting on the porch. They rushed to the pickup before he stopped.

"Mr. Joel." They gathered around him. He hugged each child.

"I'm so glad you're here. Mom's sitting on her bed just staring off into space. She won't talk to us," Wes explained.

"I tried to show her I could get my lariat to stay up, but she just said, 'That's good.'"

Cora held up her stuffed horse. "Mama didn't want horsey. Horsey makes you feel better."

The more the kids talked, the more worried he became. "Wes, why don't you tell your mom I'm in the kitchen and want to talk?"

Wes stood and raced into the house.

Joel turned to the other two children. "Todd, when I talk to your mom, would you stay outside with your sister?"

Todd nodded. "I want Mom to smile again."

"I do, too." Joel ruffled Todd's hair and brushed a kiss across Cora's forehead.

Walking into the kitchen, Joel came face-to-face with Wes.

"She's coming," he whispered.

"Stay outside with your brother and sister." Wes walked out of the kitchen.

Joel waited, not moving until April walked in. Her eyes were red and puffy. He took a step toward her, but she held up her hand.

"What's wrong, April? What happened? Did someone insult you?"

She pointed to the table. Once they were seated, she took a deep breath. "I wish it was that easy."

He wanted to assure her it was but held his tongue.

"I don't remember who asked if you wanted a baby with me," she began.

"It does—"

She held up her hand stopping him.

His heart pounded.

She took a breath. "Do you remember when I told you I wasn't going to have any more babies?"

"I do." A sick feeling started in the pit of his stomach.

"It isn't a choice, Joel. When I had Cora, I started to hemorrhage. I ended up having a hysterectomy. Physically, I cannot have any more children, and I know most men want a child of their own."

He opened his mouth to deny it, but no words came out.

She gave him a sad smile. "I didn't think you'd be able to get over that little hump. And then we hadn't discussed whether you were going to finish out the season or stay here with me to help with the harvest. But at this point, there's no need to discuss those piddling details if you can't get over the fact I can't have any more babies."

Words vanished for him as he struggled to take in what April had said. He remembered her saying she wasn't going to have any more children, but he'd thought she was just trying to make a point. He'd thought nothing of it at the time.

"It was a beautiful dream while it lasted, but I'll always know you'd never be happy not having a child of your own. Thank you for helping my children. I hope you fulfill your dream and win that belt buckle."

He wanted to argue with her that she was wrong, but suddenly he couldn't. They stood and he caught her hand. He searched her gaze for a confirmation of her words, and the sadness in her eyes told him the truth. He squeezed her hand, turned and walked out onto the porch.

"Is everything okay, Mr. Joel?" Wes asked, his face filled with worry.

Joel squatted and rested his hands on Wes's shoulders. "Not exactly." Wes wouldn't understand about wanting a child of his own, but he couldn't walk off and leave the kids without a goodbye. "Some things have come up and changed our plans. But know that I love y'all."

"What's happened? Did I do something wrong to make you mad?" Each word grew louder and louder, filled with fright.

Wes's distress ripped through him faster that an angry bull tore through a paper banner. "There's nothing you did, Wes. You, Todd and Cora are the best."

"Then why are you not staying and marrying Mom?"

The loud words brought both Todd and Cora to the porch.

"You told everyone at the cowboy church this morning you and Mom were getting married. What happened?" Tears filled Wes's eyes.

When Joel looked up, April stood outside the kitchen door, her expression as stricken as Wes's.

"Mr. Joel and I are not going to get married," April said quietly.

All the kids turned to her.

"Why, Mom?" Wes asked.

"It's complicated."

"What does that mean?" Todd demanded.

They were sinking fast.

"That means things came up," Joel answered, wanting to spare April from having to explain the situation to her kids.

Three little faces fixed on him, waiting for an explanation they would understand, but he didn't have one. He didn't understand it, either.

"What things?" Todd asked.

"Kids, say goodbye to Mr. Joel," April instructed.

If he'd kicked the kids, their expression couldn't have been filled with more pain. They simply looked at him with sad eyes, saying nothing.

He didn't know how he walked to his truck and drove off with his heart bleeding so badly. He only knew he left his heart at the ranch.

Chapter Fifteen

Joel walked from Hank's trailer with a couple of carrots on his way to see Spice.

"Hey, girl." He stood by the corral and Spice came trotting toward him. She took the carrot from his hand and chomped down.

Here was a female he understood. Well, he did understand April's reason for ending their engagement. Could he be happy just raising April's children and not have a child of his own? He didn't know.

"So why are you here talking to your horse?" Jack asked.

"I wanted to talk to a female I understood."

"I'll amen that. As long as I've been married, I've never figured out the female of the species. My wife tells me what to do and I just roll along with the demands." He studied Joel. "This have anything to do with a certain lady rancher?"

Joel ran his fingers through his hair. "Can't fool you."

"Well, I'm not Dear Abby, but even I caught how fast April left here alone." Jack waited. "Anything I can do for you?"

"No. There's nothing you or I can do to change this."

"Are you coming with us when we pull up stakes tomorrow?" Jack asked.

"As of now, I am."

Joel stared at the floor, still numb. This morning he'd been in the heights of joy. Now he was at the depths of despair.

"I hope all our celebration didn't put April off."

"No, that wasn't it. I appreciate everyone's good wishes and congratulations. It was a different issue."

"If I can help in any way, let me know." Jack walked away.

Joel wouldn't reveal April's secret.

No more babies.

Did she think him so shallow that he'd walk away from them because he wanted a child of his own? The question brought him up short.

Did it matter? He'd never thought about it until it hit him square in the face, leaving him without an answer.

"Lord, is it so wrong to want a child that is

my own? To want to pass on the family name?" His sister and her husband were expecting. But that child would be a Jensen. If he didn't have a boy of his own, there would be no more Kayes. It hadn't mattered to him before, but now?

He still could have children of his own, but not with the woman he loved. How fair was that?

He didn't know what to do.

Prayer.

He needed to talk to God. There was an answer, but he didn't know what it was.

April tucked her boys into their beds. They'd remained quiet since Joel drove off. She wondered when the questions would come.

"Mom, why did Mr. Joel leave?" Todd asked.

She knew Wes was listening.

Sitting down on Todd's bed, she said, "Well, I think Mr. Joel wanted to have babies of his own, and I can't have any more babies. He needed to know that truth before we married. It wasn't fair to him not to tell him. Half-truths are lies."

Both boys looked at her.

"Aren't we 'nough?" Todd whispered.

Her heart jerked. "You're my life and my joy. Mr. Joel—" She swallowed.

"I don't understand. If you love each other—"

"I know. It's complicated." That was a cop-out, but she didn't think Todd would understand when she didn't.

"He doesn't love us enough to stay here?"

April winced. "That's not it."

"Okay, what is it?"

"When Joel was younger, he came very close to winning a belt buckle, but his parents were killed in a car accident."

"Like our dad."

Todd's words stopped her cold. The two events were nothing alike. "Joel quit rodeoing and went home to help his younger sister with their ranch, giving up his career. Now he's very close to winning this time, and he might want to finish this year's competition and win for himself." The boys simply stared at her.

"So wouldn't he come back?"

"Yes, but—" *He might want his own children down the line and come to realize he can't live with my limitations.* That was the reason she avoided men like Joel. "It's hard to explain."

Todd rubbed his eyes. Wes refused to look at her. Her boys had gone through this disappointment before with their father, then had just recovered from the death of their grandfather. Their pain was her fault. She should've refused Joel's help in planting her fields, but how could she have done that, since it was the boys who'd hired him?

She could've at least not given in to her heart, allowing Joel to woo her and her family. The price the kids were paying was too much.

"I know it's hard now, son. But time will help."

"It's never going to be better," Todd said softly, then turned his back on her.

Wes closed his eyes and threw his arm over his face. She knew if she tried to kiss Wes goodnight, she'd make things worse. Silently, she turned off the light and left the room.

Stopping in the hall, she checked Cora. The little girl had pouted when April put her to bed.

April went to her room and lay down. Curling around one of the king-size pillows on her bed, she buried her face into its softness as the sobs came fast and hard. She'd been so lost in the happiness of falling in love, it had never occurred to her that the fact she couldn't have any more children would be a major stumbling block. But it was. No matter how she wanted it to be different, she had to face reality, again.

She'd faced Ross's desertion of his family, the deaths of her in-laws and the neglect of her parents and made it through. But this time, the circumstances cut her heart to pieces, and she didn't know if she would make it.

Why, God, have You allowed such pain into their lives? Why?

The next morning as they were doing the final packing to get on the road, Ty called out, "Joel, you've got a visitor."

His heart skipped a beat, thinking maybe

April had come to see him. Joel tied Spice to the ring on the outside of his horse trailer and walked to where Ty was helping load the calves onto the cattle truck. Wes stood there looking lost until he saw Joel and ran to him.

Wes wrapped his arms around Joel's waist.

"Is your mother here?" Joel asked.

Wes shook his head.

"How did you get here?"

"I walked."

With his mind reeling from the dangers Wes could have encountered, Joel figured the boy had to have left home at four-thirty or five o'clock.

Before Joel could say anything, Wes blurted, "I heard Mom crying last night after you left. She cried into her pillow, so's she wouldn't be heard."

Joel gently disengaged Wes from his waist, then squatted to be eye level with him.

"Is it me, Mr. Joel? Am I the reason you're not staying with us to marry Mom?" Wes's eyes filled with tears. "'Cause if that's it, I promise I'll be so good and do anything you want. I want Mama to smile and laugh again. And when you're there, she does."

All activity ceased and no one uttered a sound. Joel took a breath, looking around, seeing all the cowboys' sober expressions. They'd told him they thought he should stay with the kid and his mother. Joel searched for Millie. Maybe she could help him make Wes understand a situation that he didn't.

Joel led Wes to his trailer and sat him on the steps. Wiping the moisture from the boy's face, he said, "Wes, it is nothing you or your brother or your sister did. Your mama worried I might want another baby, and she told me she couldn't have any more babies, and if it was important to me, then I should know."

"Aren't we enough for you?"

That was the question Joel had wrestled with all night, but he still had no answer.

Joel hugged the boy. "You are a stand-up young cowboy, and any man would be proud to have you as his son."

"My dad wasn't."

Wes's answer ripped him up inside, leaving Joel to wonder if he wouldn't bleed out.

Out of the corner of his eye, Joel saw Millie blanch. He drew back and looked into Wes's face. He wanted to assure this young man that it was his father's shallowness that had caused the problem, but Wes didn't need him trashing his father.

"Wes, your dad was human, and humans make mistakes. From what I've seen of you, Todd and Cora, you are all great kids."

"We can't be that good, since you don't want to stay with us, either."

Another dagger sliced his heart.

There was no way to explain. No way to stop

the hurt or fix the situation without more hurt. Joel stepped back. "You probably haven't eaten. Let's go see Hank to see if he has anything you might like."

Wes studied the floor for a moment until his stomach growled. Joel didn't wait for an answer, but headed toward the concession stand.

"Hank, do you have anything that a hungry boy could eat?"

Hank walked out of the kitchen with a scowl on his face. "What do you—" One look at Wes brought the complaint to a halt.

"I've packed everything." After a moment, Hank said, "Wes, do you like chocolate doughnuts?"

The boy nodded.

"I've got one I've stashed away for a snack later this morning, but I think I know a young man who could use it more than me. And I'll bring you a carton of milk to wash that doughnut down with."

"Thank you," Wes whispered.

Joel sat across from Wes. "I'll need to call your mom to let her know you're safe."

Wes nodded.

Other cowboys continued to glance over at Wes. A mixture of emotions crossed their faces. Joel didn't want to do this because it would get Wes in trouble, but he couldn't have April worried. He dialed the house number. The phone didn't finish its first ring when it was picked up.

"Yes."

"April, I want you to know that Wes is here with me. He's safe."

"Oh, thank you. I was crazy worried about him."

"I can drive him out to the ranch."

"No, I'll be there and pick him up and take him on to school." She hung up.

Wes glanced up at him. "Is she mad?"

"She didn't say anything. Your mom's bringing school clothes so you can go to school. But she was very worried about you."

Hank brought the doughnut and milk and Wes paid attention to the doughnut, avoiding eye contact with anyone. The hunch of Wes's shoulders told Joel of his discouragement and his worry about what his mom might do.

"Sometimes when our moms yell at us, it's because they are scared we might have been hurt."

"Really?"

"So if your mom yells at you when she shows up, it's because she was afraid."

Wes didn't appear convinced. When he finished his doughnut and milk, he turned and asked, "Could I go and see Spice one last time? And maybe Helo and Sadie?"

Joel had left Spice tied to his trailer. "Sure, I think she might like to see you, and I know I need to bring her a treat since I left her tied up. Helo and Sadie are already in the trailer."

Joel grabbed a peppermint from Hank's stash, and they walked to where Spice stood. Wes talked to her and stroked her neck. Joel handed the boy the candy and he fed it to her.

"I'm going to miss you, girl," Wes murmured close to her ear.

Turning, Spice nudged him with her muzzle.

Wes wrapped his arms around the horse's neck and laid his head against Spice's shoulder.

Seeing how Wes interacted with the horse made Joel realize how much he cared for these children. But if he married April, he would have no sons or daughters of his own. It hadn't been an issue before, because he hadn't planned on marrying anytime soon. Until this week, he'd had no other vision in his life than winning that belt buckle. When he did marry, he'd just naturally assumed he'd have kids. His kids. But now?

He heard the pounding of feet, then April appeared, carrying Cora, Todd beside her. She put the little girl down and hugged Wes.

"Do you know what I went through when I walked into your room and didn't find you? Couldn't find you anywhere?" She choked the words past the tears clogging her throat.

Wes glanced at him and Joel raised his brow.

April pulled back. "And when you get home tonight from school, you're going to be grounded and have extra chores." She opened the big cotton bag on her shoulder and pulled out clean jeans and a shirt. "You need to change, then I'll drive you to school."

He nodded and walked to the men's restroom. She stood and tried to ignore Joel.

He stepped closer, not wanting his words to be heard by the other kids and the cowboys witnessing the scene. "Don't be too hard on him. He thought it might've been something he did that caused me to leave."

She whirled, her face drained of color. "What did you tell him?"

"I told him it wasn't his fault."

She opened her mouth to say something, but his words stopped her. "He asked if they weren't enough for me." Taking a deep breath, he struggled to get his emotions under control. "So, be gentle with him."

She nodded. "I hadn't thought."

"I've spent all night thinking about what you said, and it doesn't matter to me, April, about having more children."

Her gaze softened. "Maybe not today, Joel, but it will, and I'll always worry about it. What day will it be that you realized you made a mistake? You're a man about family. Who else would've given up their career to care for their sister?"

"You're proving my point."

She shook her head. "This time, it's different.

Until last Monday, your main goal was to win the championship buckle. You hadn't planned to quit or suddenly acquire a family. I don't want to stand in your way of a goal you'd had for a long time. If my boys hadn't hired you, you would've never thought of quitting."

He saw the fear in her face and knew she was grasping for any excuse.

Wes showed up, dressed for school.

"Let's get moving, boys. You're already late for school." She shooed them toward the door.

"April," Joel called out.

She stepped closer and cupped his cheek. "I wish you well, Joel. Let me know if you win. Thank you for all you've done for the children and me. You brought them laughter after a long time of sadness. Thank you. Take care."

Her determined stride took her away, making him realize how much he'd miss them.

"You should've fought harder," Hank said.

"You're right," Joel whispered.

That night, April sat in her room, feeling as though she'd been kicked by one of the horses. There'd been no chatter at the table tonight. Three quiet children had declined watching TV and gone to their rooms.

Her phone rang.

"What's going on?" Kelly asked. "My kids told me that your boys came to school late."

"Wes walked to the auditorium this morning to talk to Joel."

"Why would he do that?"

April swallowed. "Joel proposed to me on Sunday."

The squeal that came across the phone line made April jerk the handset away from her ear. "That's wonderful, April. So why do you sound so sad?"

"Kelly, Joel wants children of his own. I told him I couldn't have any more children. You should've seen his face." April took a couple of deep breaths to steady herself instead of breaking down and blubbering like a two-year-old. "It shattered his dreams."

"Did he say that?" Kelly demanded.

"No, but I know it would eventually matter, and if we were married and he decided he wanted children, it just wouldn't work."

"Shame on you, April Landers. You didn't give that man a chance. If he said it didn't matter, you should've believed him."

"I couldn't count on it. It would hurt us less now than if we got married and he decided he wanted children."

"From what I saw of the man, I think you could've trusted him."

"It's too late, Kelly. He's gone."

"Well, April, with that logic, you're never

going to remarry, if you can't trust a man to love you and your family."

"I know."

After agreeing to meet in town tomorrow, April hung up.

Had Kelly been right? Had she not given Joel enough credit?

It was too late now.

Chapter Sixteen

Joel flew off the bucking horse, landing hard on his back. The air whooshed out of him, making him feel as if he'd been hit with a two-by-four. Several cowboys hurried to where he lay.

"You okay?" Buck asked, looking down at him.

Joel could only nod.

Buck reached down and Joel took his hand and stood. As Joel limped out of the arena, the audience applauded. Lifting his hat, he acknowledged their concern and support.

Once out of sight, Joel dusted off the dirt clinging to his jeans.

"Your head's not in your game," Jack said as he walked toward him.

"Yeah, I did a miserable job tonight."

"Are you going to be off this stop, too? You didn't do so hot a job in Amarillo."

Joel blinked several times. He'd chalked his

poor performance up to the emotions of leaving April and the kids. He'd expected to eventually shake off the sadness, find his focus again, and his drive for the belt buckle would go back to normal. It wasn't working out that way. He couldn't get Wes's plea out of his head. Nor could he ignore the wounded look in April's eyes.

"I'd ask you what's wrong, but I don't want to appear stupid," Jack said.

Joel folded his arms across his chest. "Meaning?"

"Meaning?" Jack's eyes widened then he shook his head. "Every cowboy here knows you left your heart and your talent in Lubbock."

Joel sputtered but didn't bother to deny it.

"So you're just going to walk away without a fight? I figured you were a smarter man than that."

Joel didn't want to reveal the real reason for breaking up with April. "There are some things that can't be changed."

"Yeah, what?"

Joel patted Jack on the back. "Thanks for the concern." He moved to the far side of the gates and watched the rest of the cowboys finish their events.

After the night's performance, Joel pitched in to make sure the animals were fed, watered and settled down. He worked with a minimum of talk. When he finished, he went to his trailer.

Sitting alone, he finally accepted the truth. He'd managed to avoid reality in Amarillo by driving himself to exhaustion. But now he knew he had to deal with it.

If he wanted children of his own, he'd have to forget April and marry someone else. He'd told her not having his own kids was okay with him, but he'd said the words to keep her from walking away. She'd seen he hadn't really meant them and sent him on his way.

"Move on." The words tasted bitter on his tongue.

Could he do that? Did he want to do that?

What was a man's true legacy? Was it children? Or was it how a man lived his life and treated others? Maybe God had meant for him to love April as his wife and Wes, Todd and Cora as his children. God had known this was the family he belonged with—and to.

Someone knocked on his door.

"It's open," he called out.

The door opened and Millie stood there. She didn't enter, but placed her fists on her hips. "I thought you were a smart man."

Joel sat up straight, ready to defend himself.

"Just wipe that outraged expression from your face. Stupid is stupid, and I know you're not a stupid man. What's wrong with you?" Millie waved away the question. "Never mind. It doesn't matter. You're missing a special lady and her children. So why are you here in Wichita Falls when they are in Lubbock?"

"She's afraid."

"'Course she is."

"She's afraid I might want children of my own." He ran his fingers through his hair.

"I can understand that. To go back and have another baby when she's got the youngest out of diapers, well, that's asking a lot of a woman. I think I would've broken Mike's arm if he wanted another baby after I got all of them out of diapers."

"It isn't a choice, Millie. She can't, and she's afraid I would want a child of my own."

"Oh." That took some of the wind out of her sails. She studied him. "Do you?"

"I've purposely avoided dealing with the question until now. But after that last horse dumped me on my back and shook some sense into me…"

"You better answer that question, and quickly, because that door might not remain open."

"Thanks, Millie." He closed the door and sat on the bunk. He'd been miserable these past weeks away from April. Late at night, when things settled down around the rodeo, he could hear April's laughter and see her smile. She'd made his heart beat in a way it hadn't before. Oh, sure, she'd had her guard up when he first showed up at the ranch, but it hadn't taken long for her to lower her defenses and allow him to see the woman she was.

And he liked that woman.

Admired that woman.

Loved that woman.

And missed those boys and the little princess who wanted to be held.

But there would be no other children. Could he live with that?

He rolled the idea around in his head.

His phone rang. Joel's heart jumped. Maybe it was April. Snatching his phone, he answered. "Yes."

"Hey, big brother, how's it going?"

"Oh, it's you."

"What's that supposed to mean?" Brenda snapped.

"Sorry, sis. I was hoping you were someone else."

"Who? That rancher you worked for?"

"April. Yeah, that's who."

"You know, Joel, when you came home after the accident that killed Mom, Dad and Grandma, there were days I wanted to talk to you about my hurt, but I convinced myself I could deal with it. I couldn't."

"I'm sorry I failed you, sis."

"Talk to me, Joel. What's wrong?"

"I fell in love with a beautiful woman with three children." He explained what the issues were.

"Do you think that either Gramps or Dad would say *don't marry her*? Or Mom or Grandma? God put that woman in your path, kinda like He put Caleb in mine. And I think you belong there with April and her family. As for that belt buckle, well, you'll have to work that out with the lady. But don't walk away. You'll regret it. And there's more to my big brother than just walking away because of April's condition. Do you want to be those children's father?"

He did. "Thanks, sis. I'll let you know if you need to come out to Lubbock for a wedding."

"Call me with the answer today or tomorrow when you get back to where you should be."

He knew what to do. He found Jack.

"I'm leaving early tomorrow morning, Jack. I left something very important in Lubbock."

Jack grinned. "We were wondering how long it would take you to realize you needed to go back. Ty got it right. He's off chores for the next week."

Joel's jaw dropped. "You were wondering how long it would take? How many others are in on this?"

"To a man, we're all in."

"Thanks for telling me." Joel ran his fingers through his hair.

"It had to be your decision. We were waiting."

Jack shrugged. "Hey, we may be cowboys, but we recognize lovesickness when we see it."

Suddenly applause broke out and Joel looked around at the grinning faces of all the cowboys and those who worked with the rodeo.

At five the next morning, Joel loaded Spice in her trailer and said goodbye.

Jack clapped Joel on the back. "Get going. I think you have a family to see."

He did. His family. If they'd still have him.

April worked in the barn, checking to see what she needed and what she could afford on her limited budget. She paused, fighting back tears. She hadn't realized she'd miss Joel as much as she did. The loneliness and heartache intensified when she saw how Joel's absence affected the children. There'd been no laughter since he left.

The other day, April had overheard Cora telling her horse that she missed Daddy Joel. Her innocent comment had stolen April's breath.

Todd and Wes seemed to have had the air let out of them as they moped about. The first day after Joel left, the boys had tried to practice with their lariats. Todd had burst into tears. Wes had managed to lasso the post on the corral gate. April had applauded and tried to talk it up.

"Aren't you proud of yourself, Wes?"

He shrugged.

"Well, I'm proud of you."

"I wish Mr. Joel was here to see it."

She didn't say anything else.

She'd done the right thing, so why did it feel so wrong? Sometimes she'd wake in the middle of the night and ask God why Joel hadn't stayed.

Church folk didn't ask her what had happened, but several of the people in her Sunday school class hugged her and said they were praying for her. Last Sunday, after listing the prayer requests the pastor had added, "For all those who are dealing with grief." She felt as if a spotlight picked her out of the audience.

Kelly knew the real reason why April had ended the short-lived engagement, but her support seemed somewhat muted. April didn't understand and wasn't up to asking why.

She sat on a bale of hay in the barn. What if she'd been wrong about Joel? Maybe he'd been sent by God to be the answer to her prayers and she'd turned her back.

"Mom, Mom," Wes called out.

Before she could answer, she heard the children squeal.

"Mom, come here. Quick."

She heard Cora shriek again.

April's heart jerked. Had something happened? She raced out of the barn expecting the worst and stopped dead. Her three children jumped around, grinning and cheering.

"He's here! He's here!" Wes chanted.

Cora had her horse and yelled, "Daddy Joel!"

Todd yelled, "Yeah, he's home. Thank You, Jesus."

April didn't know whether to cheer at Todd's actions or jump up and down with the children. Instead, she stood rooted to the ground.

Joel's truck drove toward the barn. What was he doing here? His truck had his horse trailer attached.

Her heart started to pound.

Joel stopped the truck in front of the barn, opened the truck door, and the kids mobbed him.

"Mr. Joel," the kids shouted.

Wes and Todd wrapped their arms around Joel's waist and leg. He patted their backs. Cora raised her arms and he scooped her up.

She gave him a kiss on the cheek. "Missed you."

Joel did a double take. "I missed you, too. And Wes and Todd." He walked toward April. "And I missed your mama real bad."

"Why'd you go away?" Todd asked.

"Well, sometimes, we make boneheaded decisions, but I missed you so much so I came back. I'd like to make this ranch my home, because I love the beautiful woman who lives here, and I love her children. I'd like to make this family my forever family. I was wondering if she'd marry that old cowboy who needs a home."

The kids looked from Joel to April.

"Can you live with my limitations?" Her eyes locked with his. "And can you live without a championship belt buckle?" She wanted to believe, but could she trust her heart?

He smiled. "I've realized that a belt buckle can't compare with the wonderful gift that I found here. I was hired for a week, but I'd like to apply for the long-term job of husband and daddy. And no belt buckle can compare with that. Besides, I need to make sure these boys can whirl a lariat and rope a fence post."

"I got the fence post last week," Wes piped up.

Could she believe? God knows the desires of our hearts. When she'd prayed for help, He'd sent Joel. Would He have sent a man who wasn't right for her?

Joy filled April. This time she wouldn't ignore the gift she'd been given. She stepped close to Joel and he wrapped his free arm around her waist. April leaned up and whispered in his ear, "Yes."

Joel brushed a kiss across her lips.

"What did she say?" Wes asked.

"She said yes."

The boys shouted and jumped around. Cora wanted down and joined her brothers in their happy dance.

April slid her arms around Joel. "Did you know you're an answer to prayer?"

"No, but I'm glad you were praying, because

it answered a need I didn't know I had. But God knows our needs even if we don't."

"Amen."

Epilogue

"Stay still," Kelly told April as she fixed the flowers in April's hair. "You're worse than my Becky, who can't sit still for two minutes for me to put her hair in a ponytail."

"Well, I feel as excited as Becky. Or it could be your growing stomach you can't see around." April took a deep breath, wanting to pinch herself to see if this was really happening. She was getting married again. Something she'd never thought would occur. But an amazing thing had happened. Her heart and soul had been healed. Just when she'd abandoned all hope and known she couldn't do it all by herself, she'd let go and let God step in.

Funny how that worked.

This past month had seen so many changes in their lives. April looked at her friend in the mirror. "Without everyone at church pitching in, we never could've pulled off this wedding.

And without you directing everyone, it wouldn't have happened. You may have discovered a new career."

"It was fun to do this for you, but I don't know if I'd want to do this on a regular basis." Kelly gave April a hug. "It's the least I could do for my friend. Besides with all the hormones flowing through my veins, Dave's grateful I'm focused on something else besides him leaving his muddy jeans on the bedroom carpet. The man is worse than the kids."

April laughed.

The door to the small room opened and Joel's sister, Brenda, walked in carrying Cora. Her little girl had a circle of flowers surrounding her head, with colorful ribbons flowing down the back.

"Look, Mama, I have flowers."

Standing, April walked to her daughter and made a production of studying Cora. "You are beautiful."

Cora grinned. "Yes."

"Thank you," April whispered to Brenda.

Brenda hugged April. "No, I should thank you. I see the special sparkle in my brother's eyes. He deserves happiness. You and your children are just right for him, and he'll be as faithful with you as he was with me. That's his heart."

"I love Daddy Joel," Cora announced.

Brenda teared up and wiped her eyes. "You

know, for an ex–army captain, I cry like a two-year-old."

"It's all those hormones. I know." April smiled.

A knock sounded at the door and the pastor's wife leaned in. "Are you ready?"

More than anyone would know. "I am."

Joel stood at the front of the church watching the double doors.

"When are they getting here?" Wes asked, pulling at his string tie. His new Western coat matched his brother's.

Joel glanced down at his two groomsmen, Wes and Todd. These were his sons and he couldn't think of anyone better to stand as his groomsmen.

Before Joel could answer, the organ strains sounded through the church and the doors opened. Cora stood there with her basket of flower petals and behind her stood Brenda and Kelly. When the music started Cora skipped down the aisle, her basket on her arm, throwing out rose petals. When she saw Millie, she waved and threw rose petals on her. Millie smiled and encouraged Cora to continue to the front of the church. After several more steps, Cora stopped, threw down her basket and made a beeline to Joel. He scooped her up. Brenda and Kelly followed behind Cora with a little less drama. His sister gave him a wink.

The music swelled and the first notes of the wedding march rang through the sanctuary. His bride and Caleb Jensen, his brother-in-law, stood at the end of the aisle. Caleb would escort April down the aisle since her father couldn't get away from his job in Brazil and her mother had a reception with the president of the country she'd chosen not to miss. But April's expression only held joy.

Watching her walk toward him, Joel felt a tightening in his throat. His heart swelled with love and gratitude. God had given him a ready-made family, one he couldn't have imagined, but one he'd always be grateful for. And no championship buckle could ever compare.

* * * * *

Dear Reader,

I hoped you enjoyed Joel and April's story. When Joel first appeared in his sister's book, I knew I'd have to tell his story. Have you ever missed an opportunity or dream, then been given a second chance to go for it? Joel found himself in that position. He was now living his dream, but something was missing. And he didn't know what until he encountered a lovely widow with her two rambunctious little boys and charming baby girl.

April was determined to avoid being hurt again by a man who couldn't stay in one place, which had been the case in her first marriage. Little did she know that the traveling cowboy who showed up at her back door was just what she'd prayed for.

Wes, Todd and Cora stole my heart. I hope they stole yours, too.

Sometimes answers to our prayers are given, just not in the way we think they should be answered. Both Joel and April realize that truth, and once they let go of their preconceived notions, they found their answers. I've found that in my life letting go and letting God have His way brings us our heart's desire.

Leann Harris

LARGER-PRINT BOOKS!

GET 2 FREE
LARGER-PRINT NOVELS
PLUS 2 FREE
MYSTERY GIFTS

Love Inspired®

SUSPENSE
RIVETING INSPIRATIONAL ROMANCE

Larger-print novels are now available...

YES! Please send me 2 FREE LARGER-PRINT Love Inspired® Suspense novels and my 2 FREE mystery gifts (gifts are worth about $10). After receiving them, if I don't wish to receive any more books, I can return the shipping statement marked "cancel." If I don't cancel, I will receive 4 brand-new novels every month and be billed just $5.49 per book in the U.S. or $5.99 per book in Canada. That's a savings of at least 19% off the cover price. It's quite a bargain! Shipping and handling is just 50¢ per book in the U.S. and 75¢ per book in Canada.* I understand that accepting the 2 free books and gifts places me under no obligation to buy anything. I can always return a shipment and cancel at any time. Even if I never buy another book, the two free books and gifts are mine to keep forever.

110/310 IDN GH6P

Name	(PLEASE PRINT)	
Address		Apt. #
City	State/Prov.	Zip/Postal Code

Signature (if under 18, a parent or guardian must sign)

Mail to the **Reader Service:**
IN U.S.A.: P.O. Box 1867, Buffalo, NY 14240-1867
IN CANADA: P.O. Box 609, Fort Erie, Ontario L2A 5X3

Are you a current subscriber to Love Inspired® Suspense books and want to receive the larger-print edition?
Call 1-800-873-8635 or visit www.ReaderService.com.

* Terms and prices subject to change without notice. Prices do not include applicable taxes. Sales tax applicable in N.Y. Canadian residents will be charged applicable taxes. Offer not valid in Quebec. This offer is limited to one order per household. Not valid for current subscribers to Love Inspired Suspense larger-print books. All orders subject to credit approval. Credit or debit balances in a customer's account(s) may be offset by any other outstanding balance owed by or to the customer. Please allow 4 to 6 weeks for delivery. Offer available while quantities last.

Your Privacy—The Reader Service is committed to protecting your privacy. Our Privacy Policy is available online at www.ReaderService.com or upon request from the Reader Service.

We make a portion of our mailing list available to reputable third parties that offer products we believe may interest you. If you prefer that we not exchange your name with third parties, or if you wish to clarify or modify your communication preferences, please visit us at www.ReaderService.com/consumerschoice or write to us at Reader Service Preference Service, P.O. Box 9062, Buffalo, NY 14240-9062. Include your complete name and address.

LISLP15